Echoes and Dreams

Robert Kibble

This collection of short stories comprises successes up to 2015. Two of these stories appeared in Writers' Forum magazine, one won the Nottingham Writers Competition, 1 was printed in an anthology by Transmundane Press, and two more were placed or commended in competitions, while another five were selected for publication online.

0

Contents

Detachment	5
Getting Away	21
Harvest Festival	31
Hind Etin	37
Home Run	41
Memories Without Echoes	44
Good Call	53
Echo of the Storm	58
Strangeness on a Train	69
Stranger Stranger	79
Survivor Guilt	90
The Girl Of Our Dreams	96
The Texture Of The Trees	117
Troll Bridge	134
Jerusalem Wormwood	140

First published in "Infective Ink" fiction website.

Detachment

"Oh come on, it's an obvious suicide."

I didn't agree. Two days ago the Chief was supporting my suspicion, saying 'trust your instincts,' but with no hard evidence his interest had faded quickly. It didn't feel right to me, though.

I'd had three dead retired doctors and two dead retired teachers, all dying in the same way. Each one seemed genuine; each one seemingly unconnected. In each case friends reported they'd been losing their marbles, at least to some degree, but maybe they knew enough to take their own lives. In each case they'd taken two pills to do it.

It felt different for this guy, though. He'd lived on his own for years, and he barely knew anyone – at least that's what the neighbours told me. They thought he must have moved away. He wasn't found for three weeks. In the end he was reported by squatters – amazingly civically-responsible squatters, by their standards, who'd found him when they broke in and phoned us. If he hadn't had a pretty amazing-looking house right on the corner of the Oxford Road I wonder if anyone would ever have found him. Presumably after some time the whole body just gets consumed somehow and any smell stops? I heard a radio programme about people who research it, but they didn't tell me what actually happens, apart from the fact that it all starts in the ears, nose and throat. Well, they said orifices, strictly speaking, but I think that's horror enough.

He – my obvious-suicide-according-to-the-Chief – was a refugee from World War Two, over here from Poland and had always hoped to return. At least that's the story his friend told me. I found that friend – another Pole called Marcin – because he'd sent a Christmas card. Our suicide left it on the mantelpiece. We found him in April. The card had a scrawled phone number, so I'd rung it.

Marcin officially identified the body, which made our lives easier.

I walked round the dead man's house looking, and wondering. It was a magnificent house, built on three stories with a basement below, and grand hallways. It would have been amazing in its time – some kind of townhouse for the lah-de-dah set, perhaps. Not much of a garden, but maybe that had been sold off. The houses behind looked new.

Anyway, something about it troubled me. I've got a habit of looking round for things which don't fit. He had piles of newspapers spread around in what had probably been some kind of larder, but that was normal enough. Some of the papers were folded to the crossword page. And some, not the ones on top, but a few inches down, were filled in. A bit higher up, and occasional clues were filled in, but not many. A few of the top ones weren't even turned to that page.

What hit me, though, was when I found an iPhone.

Not normal for that age-group. It had long since discharged, so I had to wait until I got back to the station to charge it up again and switch it on. Fortunately there was no screen lock. He'd made no more than half a dozen phone calls on it ever, unless he'd deleted them. I went through the numbers anyway. One was to Marcin, which hadn't been answered. One was to the council, who didn't have records detailed enough to help. All the others were to mobiles. I looked up the numbers, and those phones were anonymous. Bought for cash. Turned out this phone had been bought for cash too.

My boss said open-and-shut, and being a nightmare of a boss when he gets riled, that really meant that was it. I didn't have any more time, so I left it at that. But on a whim, I kept the iPhone. Just slipped it away, since no one would notice – we lose things all the time round here. I was going to go through it more thoroughly later. Not the calls, though – there was nothing there. Something else. If you made that few calls, why did you have such an expensive phone? Why not a standard one, or one of those ones with the big buttons, specially designed for the elderly?

I went through the apps he had: FreeNagram, an anagram-helper; Gnudoku, a Sudoku thing; FastLaneBrainTrain, which I'd heard of on some documentary saying it was being pushed to people who were worried about getting dementia; and OSMand, a free GPS app. Why would he need that? Where was he going? He didn't have a car, for heaven's sake.

There were some other apps that I thought were standard, but something still felt wrong about the whole thing.

I told my wife I felt suspicious, and she gave me that look that she gives when she thinks I'm "thinking too much." I told Dad about the apps too, and he recognised the name FastLaneBrainTrain, and said he had a copy as well.

"It measures your brain-age," he told me over tea one day when he'd come over to see my kids and was making clear he was only tolerating me. "Lets you know how fit your brain is. I've got the mind of someone your age. You should try it."

Yeah, I thought, so you can feel superior when mine comes out as older than yours and I feel even worse about dropping out of Uni. Some of us don't think in maths and word puzzles.

Dad went off and I did let it lie, at least until the next cadaver I found with the same poisons, a few months later. They called them the "two pills": amusingly for Matrix fans a red one and a blue one. Together they delivered a fast-acting barbiturate followed by a massive dose of sedative, so you fell asleep and your heart stopped. The Swiss had developed it, but some guys in Oregon had perfected the combination. It was what they gave to people who wanted to be able to end their own lives on their own terms. And there was absolutely nothing to make anyone suspicious about any of these cases.

Except I was suspicious.

These people had been alone, and they made that decision one day. Did they have a sudden reawakening when they realised what was happening? All of them? Or did someone slip by and help them out? Which was still a crime, even if I might grudgingly approve, given how much Dad always spoke of the fact that I'd have to "help him" if things ever got that way. And if the police don't investigate and prosecute crimes… well, that'd be like the eighties all over again.

And besides, how would they know where to get them? OAPs weren't usually big into the drug scene.

On the side I went to a doctor to ask about dementia, asking how quickly it becomes something the patient himself isn't aware of. How quickly are you beyond "oh, I'm a bit forgetful," and onto the "are you one of my children as well?" stage? Of course it varied so much that it was useless to ask.

But I did mention that inquiry to Dad, when again he came over on the pretext of catching up with his daughter-in-law, who'd been out on his last visit, although he spent no time talking to her at all. Mostly he spent the morning showering the kids with presents, including giving me a bag of a few things "for future birthdays – just in case." Yes, I mentioned my query into dementia to him, and he gave me a look I hadn't seen before. A look as if he had to stop and think, and was being guarded. A look I saw on suspects' faces every day, but I'd never seen on his.

I didn't say anything, and I'm poker-faced enough to think he wouldn't have noticed. I spent a little while working over the conversation in my head – I even made a few notes in a notebook, although for obvious reasons not my official one, and I realised I'd mentioned the app again. The FastLaneBrainTrain one. What had I said? "I tell you, Dad – the week I've had I'd be well over your age on that brain train game by now." That was all. He just clammed up.

After lunch he'd started playing with the kids again, and I'd gone to make tea. We have a loud kettle. A loud kettle can hide a multitude of sins, from tidying up spills on the floor to uncorking a bottle of whisky when the day has been stressful. I slipped out and grabbed his phone from his jacket. An iPhone – yes I know that doesn't count as coincidence in this day-and-age. A few apps alongside FastLaneBrainTrain. Nothing which matched. I looked through his calls list, and all but one had contact names associated with them. I noted the number down, and put the phone away. I'm not proud, but I felt something was up, and I got back before the kettle boiled, so no one was any the wiser.

I abused the system the next day and checked the number I'd found on Dad's phone. It had been bought for cash, as the ones on the other mobile had been, but this time there had been a top-up, with a name. I checked that name in our records.

Dead.

I asked for the post-mortem, and when I received the envelope a few days later a part of me looked at it and knew what it contained, while the other was telling me not to open it at all. Two paths, in a wood. I took the one sadly inevitable...

I opened it.

Same two pills.

So did Dad know something about this?

A couple of days later I found some free time, and went round to his. For the first time in years, in fact. I didn't normally visit, because it wasn't me he wanted to see. He didn't come to ours to see me – he wanted to see the generation that still had hope, the ones who hadn't failed. "You've got a more child-friendly house, so it's easier," had been the excuse, but I understood. This time it was different. This time he was seeing me.

"Hi."

"We didn't...?" he said, looking momentarily confused.

"No. Can I come in?"

He looked back into the house, and seemed as if he was about to say no, before relenting. He actually said "s'pose". I almost burst out laughing. The surly teenager was still in there, being asked to let someone into his room. In an instant the parent-child relationship had switched.

His house was a mess. Nothing catastrophic, but just a little mess here, and a little mess there. Hairs building up in places there shouldn't be hairs. Dust on things which had gone beyond "yeah, I know, dusting's a pain," and gone to "honestly, the treasure of the Sierra Madre might be under there." And there he was, suddenly smaller. My father. The man who'd brought me into the world, and who'd been my inspiration and my world when I was small, and for the first time in my life I realised I was taller than he was. He sat down quickly and asked me what I wanted.

"You called someone. Someone you don't know."

"What? Have you been spying on me?" and then a moment later, "Did I tell you this?"

A glass shattered. A world. My father, so much more than I would ever be, and there was doubt in his eyes. I wished I hadn't come. I wished I'd never seen this. The world that had shattered was mine.

"No. Yes. I mean, your mobile number came up in an investigation. Someone who died called you. I didn't recognise the name."

He looked relieved. Well, half-relieved. "You mean Billy?"

William, but yes. "Yes."

"He's gone, then. Peacefully, at least."

He looked at me, and looked down.

"Peacefully?" I asked. "Did you have anything… I mean, were you…" and then I stopped. I was ashamed of even starting, and only because it was my father did I talk so stupidly without thinking. Of course he couldn't. Could he? No. This was my father. My now-smiling father.

"No, no, no," he said, seeming himself again. "Did you come here because you need to know for work, or because you want to?"

I thought for a while, but I knew the answer immediately – it just took a while to filter through to my conscious brain. "I want to."

"Well, you're my son, and I trust you," he began, and in an instant my heart melted. It wasn't what he said – it was the way he said it. He meant it, absolutely. No conditions, no consulting my opinion, just saying how things were. And from that point on, he proved himself right.

"Turns out," he said, giving a half-laughing-cough, "that it was more like he had a stake in my death." He looked straight at me, maybe wondering how I was going to take it. "He knew of a pill…"

"Two pills," I interrupted. Stupidly, I knew, the moment I said it.

He smiled again. "It looks like two pills to you people. It's one to us. And it's got wifi." He laughed. "A bionic killer tapeworm."

I stared. "What?"

"That's how Billy described it to me. It attaches to your gut and then connects to the brain games thing you found. What was its name again?" He thought for a moment, eyes suddenly wistful, before shaking his head and continuing. "If I fail to get below seventy for a week in a row…" He paused, but I was in no mood to interrupt now. "…it triggers something which releases all the non-organic stuff and begins dissolving. A few days later, after plenty of time for the electronic stuff to have been flushed away…"

"…you absorb the chemicals?"

"Yes."

"But that's…"

"What I want." He stared right into my eyes, and the man I'd idolised all these years was back. But that moment was fleeting. He withered again, even as I was looking at him.

"It's not right."

"Really?" He slumped down into his favourite chair.

For a while I didn't think he was going to say any more, but he did, quieter than before, and now as if he was reading a script rather than coming up with it spontaneously, like he'd practiced this.

"We spoke about this time, and you promised to help."

I started to interrupt, but he raised a finger. Just the index finger on his right hand, but it was enough. He wasn't looking at me now; his head had slumped forward slightly. He looked so frail.

"You promised to help. Well, I know you can't. And I think you wouldn't. Don't say it, because I don't want to know I'm wrong now. I'm fading. I visit you when I'm on a good day, and I use the app to remind me to come. It's set up to tell me when I'm having a good day." He looked up, and a weak smile crossed his face.

I stared into his eyes, and went and got the phone. He sounded as if he was about to object, but his eyes drifted back to looking out of the window. I opened the app and scrolled down to the scores. It had a long-term average, and a graph, with a line across marking seventy. Mostly he'd been well below, but the last eight days were all above, with today's being the closest. The ones before were well above. "You've already failed?"

"What?" He looked as if he was about to fall asleep.

"You've failed?" I ran round in front of him. "You've been over seventy for a week!"

He looked into my eyes, tears welling up in his. I'd never seen him cry. "I think so, yes."

"It's released? I can get help…"

He surfaced for a moment, reoccupying his eyes. "Cut me open? No. No, son. I made my choice, months ago, and it's right. Look at me. You can remember this, but the kids? I want them to remember me as something else. As something I was. As what I," he said, putting a weak hand to his chest, "always am in here…"

I looked at him, not knowing what to say. Some part of him had gone, to be sure, but he was my father. "I can come every day."

He looked up at me again, and the smile was wider. Tears did flow down his face. "I won't come to you again. But I'd like you to come here. At least find me quickly. And, son…"

"Yes, Dad?"

"Give me a hug."

I squatted down and held him gently, and I felt his head fall forward onto my shoulder. He felt so light in my arms. I pulled back after a while, and his eyes were shut. For a moment I panicked, and checked his pulse, but he was obviously still breathing.

"Good-bye, Dad," I said as I left, just in case.

I took his spare key.

He struggled to recognise me the next day, and kept asking if I was going to get married, saying what a lucky girl she'd be, whoever she was.

The day after, he was dead. I found him, and I reported him. I hid the phone, of course.

My boss was suspicious at first, given the interest I'd shown, but he convinced himself there just had to be some website advertising something, and lost interest after a few days, after Dad was buried. My wife cried more than I did.

I guess I'd said my goodbye.

Winner of the 2015 Nottingham Writers' Newcomer Short Story Prize

Getting Away

"Bye, love. Thanks for the lift." Sue looked at her watch. "I need to dash." She jumped out of the car and ran into the station, holding her handbag above her head in a futile attempt to keep her hair dry.

Dave didn't have time to reply. As he watched her reach the station doors his mind ran through why she hadn't rung a taxi earlier on a busy Friday night, and how much of the snooker he was missing, and then back to Tom. It would have been an effort to wake him up and get him into the car, and it would have taken longer, but still – it was wrong to leave him. And from now until he got home, Dave knew that would be a constant worry.

There was a jam on the way out of the car park. The rain was so heavy cars were having trouble seeing when the road was clear. It really was a horrible night. Dave waited his turn, trying to be calm, but found his fingers turning white, tightly gripping the steering wheel. "Come on, people," he said, quietly. "Come on."

I'm still tired. What woke me? I feel sore. I'm hungry. I want something to eat.

He knew it was bad to leave, but it should only have been half an hour. Sue wanted to get away for her girly weekend. She needed to get away, truth be told. The last few months had been hard. Tom wasn't easy to cope with. A weekend away would recharge her batteries, and Dave owed her that. It left him to cope alone, but he could do that. Just so long as he got home.

Just so long as Tom didn't wake up and panic, or get out.

Oh God. Get out.

Without thinking any more Dave pushed on his horn, willing the car in front of him to get out of the way. They were all turning right, into town, but they were all positioning themselves in the road so they blocked him. He was going left, out of town to the tiny village where they'd lived for the last few years.

The car ahead wiped its rear windscreen, and Dave could just see the woman's eyes looking back at him in the mirror. She looked upset.

"I'm sorry," said Dave, knowing his words wouldn't reach her. "But can you please get out of my way. I need to get home."

He knew it was wrong to come out and leave Tom, but surely just once…

Should there be someone here? I want food. Someone should bring me food.

The road ahead cleared and he moved forward, a bit too fast. He blamed the overly-sensitive clutch.

The road to the left was empty, and he sped up, turning the wipers onto double speed. It still didn't clear enough. He leaned forward to see better, and opened his window a crack to stop the car steaming up. A few hundred yards later and the streetlights stopped. Dave turned his lights to main beam, and then realised it only lit up the rain, so turned them back again and slowed down a little.

Another car turned out into the road and headed towards him. Dave slowed a bit more, concentrating on the cat's eyes in the middle of the road to make sure he was in the right place. If he looked up directly at the other car, he'd be blinded. He slowed more, and the car sped past, going way faster than he was.

Dave took a deep breath and sped up again. The glass of wine he'd had earlier, thinking he was settled, felt as if it was smothering his brain, dulling him. If Sue hadn't needed to go – really needed – he would have refused to drive. It was probably OK. One glass – that was OK, right? If only she'd rung up before the Friday evening rush.

He turned into the smaller road that led directly to his house. Only two miles to go, he thought, as he drove through a gigantic puddle. The spray either side reached up above the side windows, and the car slid a little. Dave changed down to second gear, and continued on.

No one is here. Where is she? I'm so hungry. I need to find her. I should shout. She will come.

One more dip between him and home. He could take the other road and go the higher way round, but it was only a couple of minutes now – he could make it home, and check that Tom was all right. Just check on him. Tom would still be asleep, of course. Everything would be fine. Just a couple of minutes.

A lake appeared in front of him where the road should have been. He tried to work out how deep it would be, but you couldn't tell in the darkness. Dave changed down to first gear and kept going, feeling the car straining against the water, producing a wash that burst up over the bonnet. It was all about keeping the revs up, and keeping the speed down. He knew that. He pushed on, keeping his foot half-down on the pedal, using the clutch now and again to get a full set of revs on. The car pushed forward, and he felt the slight change of incline as he reached the lowest point.

The engine spluttered. He pushed down on the pedal,

but it was no use. The sound of the car stopped.

"No. Please, no. Not today."

He turned the key, and felt a little water seep in under the door. The key did nothing.

Dave slammed his fists into the steering wheel again. He took his phone out, and swiped it. No signal.

"Shit shit shit."

There was nothing for it.

He pushed the handle on the door, and let the water flood in over his feet. Swivelling out he pushed his feet down into the foot-deep water. It was freezing.

As an afterthought he leaned back in and turned on the hazard lights, not that anyone else would be stupid enough to come along this road in this, unless they were a four-by-four. He'd always taken the mickey out of the people with the Chelsea tractors, but not now. What he'd give for that.

Dave pulled his feet along through the water, following the line of the road with eyes wide open, staring into the blackness, cursing his lack of jacket. He was soaked through in seconds, but at least as he went along the water became shallower, until he was walking in waterlogged shoes but at least on dry land. Well, dry-ish land anyway.

He thought of Tom, wondering where he was, and kept going. He tried to run, but his feet wouldn't do it. He shivered as he walked, and he felt his shirt sticking to him, with the wind blowing past draining all the heat from his upper body.

I can't find anyone. Maybe she's outside. The door is locked. I can reach the key.

The turns of the road which were normally seconds apart took minutes, and it felt like an hour to get the last mile, until he could just see the house.

He wanted to make out the windows, and the lights, to check it was all as he'd left it. That was all that mattered. He could have a bath. He could throw the shoes away. He could phone the AA tomorrow and get the car pulled out. Just so long as Tom was where they'd left him.

Upstairs windows, lights were off.

Downstairs, one on, one off.

The door. It was dark, and Dave had to stare a couple of times, but there was something wrong.

It was open.

Oh God no.

Dave summoned every ounce of strength he had and began running, his legs trying to refuse, but being overruled by a now-desperate heart, needing to get to that house. Perhaps it had only been seconds ago, he thought. Perhaps half an hour.

He raced up to the house and looked round. No sign. Perhaps Tom had simply found the key and opened the door. Perhaps he was still inside.

Dave shouted, and looked quickly in the downstairs room, where Tom had been sleeping. Gone.

He ran back out again, and started round the house. The side gate was open – he should have noticed that immediately. The garden was long, and led down to a stream – a stream which would by now be a torrent of water.

He pushed on again, now through mud. Surely Tom couldn't have made it out through this, and why would he stay out?

He ran down towards the stream, staring at the ground wondering if there were footprints or not. It was too dark and too slimy to tell.

He slipped and fell on his back, mud splattering over him as he turned and tried to get up again.

A deep breath, realising how numb his hands were as he tried to use them to stand, and he got back to his feet. "Tom!" he shouted.

Someone is shouting. I'm wet. I'm cold. I don't like this. I'm still hungry.

Dave didn't expect a response.

He half-ran half-crawled down to the bottom of the garden, and then saw him.

Dave almost fell to his knees as he saw the man, standing there, but kept upright enough to get to him. "Dad!"

"I was looking for Carol," said Tom.

Dave threw his arms round his father, his tears lost in the rain. As he held him he felt the shivering body, and wondered when he last hugged his father. Not since he was little.

A young man is holding me. He's warm. Where's Carol?

"Is Carol with you?"

Dave turned his father back towards the house, ignoring the question. His mother had been dead twelve years now.

"We need to get you warm."

The cold flooded over him, but he pushed on back towards the house, gently guiding Tom back into the house. He would need to be warmed up too, before Dave would have a chance to sneak up to the shower. Plus the mud would be all over the house from his racing round earlier.

Still, none of that mattered. Never again, he promised. Never again.

First published in "Every Day Fiction" fiction website.

Harvest Festival

Thank you for coming. Please sit down. First I need to tell you that we are going to kill you today.

Yes, I am quite serious. I'm sorry to have to tell you, but there is no question about how this day is going to end for you, and the quicker you get used to that the better. You have had a life, and we're going to go over exactly what that was, but you need…

No, really. This is happening. Look into my eyes, and you will see I am not joking.

Why? Well, because, because you are a clone, and your body is needed now.

Yes. Really.

You are going to die. Today. I really need you to understand that, Mr Green. To accept it, because only when you've done that can we move on.

Yes, Mr Green, that's a good question, and one everyone asks.

Yes, everyone. Everyone you have known who left the compound went through exactly what you are going through now. Which is to say, they were all used for rehousing their owners' brains.

Yes, that's fine Mr Green. You can't do anything about it, and if shouting helps, that's fine, although we have taken the precaution of drugging you, so you won't be able to damage the body. We need it, you see. Only your head will be able to move in a few seconds. That gives us enough time to talk.

Of course we have something to talk about, Mr Green, because believe it or not, this is a voluntary scheme. How do you think we got authorisation for it? The clones – you – must live a luxurious enough life prior to harvesting that you yourselves approve the scheme.

Oh, come come now, Mr Green. Don't be like that. Let's just sit back and have a bit of a think about what's happened in your life, shall we?

You were born and accelerated, with memories implanted, but that's only the early years. Everything from six years old is genuine. So, let's go through it, shall we?

Yes, it really is important, and yes, you are going to die today.

And yes, I can wait for you to stop screaming. Mr Green, please calm down.

No, there's nothing I can do to you more than killing you, but we have to ask you some questions, and we have to set the scene first. So…

…

…thank you.

So, everything from six was genuine. Your gang at school was real, and your friends were real. Mark was harvested, which is why you never heard from him again. His owner was hit by a car at the age of fourteen, which is a very unusual occurrence, it has to be said. He voted against continuing the programme, which is always disappointing. But returning to you, that crush you had on Wendy – that was real. That was the two of you, enjoying your young lives. Your first kiss was real. Joan at the end of the school sports day – that was real. You lived, and you loved, and you enjoyed real connections with other human beings.

No, Mr Green, that doesn't make it worse.

I'm getting to that. I just want to go through another couple of events in your life.

Your films. They were amazing, and people outside the compound have enjoyed them. Your owner was even impressed, and has taken a media course thinking he might have innate talent, although I do wonder if this is where clones…

Yes, your owner. He knows about your life.

Oh, that's what you're going to focus on now? Mr Green, with all due respect, you're living in an artificial compound where we've lied about the global contagions, and we're going to kill you to transplant your owner's brain into your body, and you're worried about surveillance?

There. That's better. Well, not better as such. But we're back, aren't we?

Yes, Mr Green. You need to stop shouting again.

I understand being paralysed isn't pleasant, but I can reassure you that you will die very painlessly indeed. If that helps.

No no, it very rarely does, that's true. It seems odd to me, though – I'd have thought it would be quite important, once we've settled that you are dying in… oh, around twenty minutes time.

Yes, Mr Green, there is something important to do. We have to ask you a very important question. It's a matter of approval.

No, Mr Green, I've told you. You are going to die. That's been decided.

Yes, approval. And since you're not going to get calmer, I should tell you from this point there will be an official government observer to this conversation, and I need to tell you the question.

Yes, the question I brought you in here to answer.

Do you accept your life was worthwhile, and therefore give approval for two future clones, unrelated to you or your owner, being created, living their lives in luxury, and then if needed being harvested for their owners?

It's a very important question, that's what kind of question it is.

And that, Mr Green is a good question. What do you have to gain? The answer I'm afraid is nothing. But if you think your life was good enough to have been worth living, then it follows it is worth it for others. For other people's clones to live in the compound.

I think you will, yes. Because think of the alternative. It isn't that you live a long and free life. The alternative is that you never lived at all. And the two clones you'd be approving – would it be better for them to have the life you've had, with all its ups and downs, and your absolutely-real connections to Wendy, and Joan, and all your friendships…? Or would you rather not have been at all? That, Mr Green, is the question. So, before we make your body available for your owner, and for the record, do you give approval?

First published in "Farnham Flash Fiction" anthology of longlisted entries.

Hind Etin

Mother?

Darling?

Be quiet. He doesn't know I'm here.

What are you doing?

I can get you out. Out of this cage.

No. He made it with magic. I know there's no escape.

There is, Mother. I found it. I can free you.

Then do. Do it now. We can run away together. Oh, my darling boy I always knew you were different.

No, Mother.

What? You don't want to free me? Or you're not different? You are, my dearest. You would never do what he has done to me. You are my one consolation. The one thing he has done which isn't poison. Come here. Let me hold you.

No, Mother. You don't understand. I can free you.

So you said. Come here.

I need to explain. Before you decide.

What's there to decide? To stay here, trapped forever at his mercy?

I can't free you in this time.

What do you mean?

I can send you back. To your time. To when you decided to enter this forest. To when you didn't believe your father. To when you were young and naïve. To when you were the happy young woman I wish I could have known.

To before all this? Why wouldn't I... Oh. You mean before you? You would...

I would never be. I would never have been. Nor would my brothers, of course.

But you. You are my joy.

And you are my pain, Mother. Trapped here, and he will never release you. You know that. And I will never leave, because I will never leave you. But I can send you back. I will never have been. I will never be. You can enjoy your life, free from all this.

Please don't make me decide. I can't. To stop you ever having been born? You are my joy. Why can't you leave me, run away, make a life for yourself? I will gladly stay here and endure if you go.

You know why, Mother. The same reason you find this hard, but it's right. I will never have been. I will suffer no pain, feel nothing, have no regrets. If you stay, I can never forgive myself, my father… Or you.

Me?

You can stop this. You can stop him. You can go back and tell your father to burn down this whole wood. This never needs to happen again. You know how many young women have wandered in here? Do you know how he brags about them, about capturing them, raping them, torturing them? You can make that end.

But you…

I will not be born. You will remember me. That is enough.

Come here, my darling.

You have decided. That is good. I love you, Mother.

I love you too, my soon-to-be-unborn-child. When will it…?

Winner of the "Writers' Forum" flash fiction competition, wherein you rolled a random selection of prompts and had to write a story. My random prompts were: "Traveller / SalesPerson", "Pink-Haired / Unsuccessful", "End of an era", "Sports stadium", "Ancient spellbook".

Home Run

"Hey." A voice, uncomfortably-close. I turned to see an overweight black man, standing two feet from me, sporting insanely-dyed purple hair. "Leaving tomorrow?"

"How'd you know?" I was taking my last tour of my adopted city, standing outside Busch Stadium, home of the Cardinals.

"You been in there?"

I looked up at the stadium. I had. I'd seen McGwire break the home run record. I'd touched the baseball as it flew into the crowd, almost breaking my finger. The guy who caught it made a million dollars. I'd touched it. If I'd been one seat to the right…

"A few games." I turned. He was gone.

Grand Union Station contained my final farewell. The

"Have A Nice Day Café", where I'd spent way too long at the bar recently. It was time to leave. The novelty had worn off.

I stood at the doorway, wondering whether to go in and have one last drink. Maybe she would be there – the gorgeous girl who'd worn the silver top when I first saw her. I'd bought her a drink via the barmaid, but hadn't the guts to talk to her. I regretted that immediately, knowing I'd never have a better opportunity. I sat in a booth, and the purple-haired black guy sat down opposite.

"Regrettin' her, are you?"

I knew he knew. "Yeah."

"I can send you back."

"What?"

"Back one year. You can do it again. And do it right."

As he spoke I didn't doubt it for a second. I stared into his eyes and saw power.

To go back? To sit one to the right and catch the ball? To go over and talk to the silver-top girl first time, so it didn't become a monkey on my back? To know that all the stress of finding an apartment would be fine in the end, leaving me with a view of the St Louis Arch?

But then I'd be doing it all again. Why not just learn from what I've done, remember it, take it home?

I shook my head, and pushed my beer away. I took one last look at the silver girl. The next time I see someone like you, I told myself, I will buy you a drink in person.

And I meant it.

On the way out the black man opens the door for me and smiles. "You'll be fine," he said.

And I will.

Memories Without Echoes

The weirdest thing was I thought I heard someone's voice, someone familiar, just for a second.

It went dark, and I froze. There was a distinct click, and then nothing.

Not just the nothing you normally get on a quiet night, no. Nothing. Properly nothing. This was an anechoic chamber, used for accurate measurements of sounds. Even though I knew the sound couldn't escape, I still shouted: "Come on! Open the door!"

Could it have just fallen shut? I thought I'd left it hooked properly when I came in, but I couldn't picture the hook. I was pretty sure the tag had been there, though. Yes, the tag, making sure someone would check the room before locking up, was definitely hanging where it should have done.

Right, someone will be coming round to lock up. Just stay calm. Just breathe normally. Ignore the fact that this place is basically airtight.

Why tonight of all nights? Tonight, the night when my drop-dead-gorgeous once-and-future girlfriend Janey is finally coming back to me? She'll be heading down from Glasgow, and she'd expect me to be waiting for her. We didn't actually arrange that, but she'd expect it. Still, she knows where my parents' place is if I'm not there. She was there before, after all. That wonderful weekend.

Oh come on, someone, open the damn door.

Right, which way is the door? Have I moved since it shut? I only came in to change one of the foam cones, and I was going to leave. For a bank holiday weekend of unadulterated joy. I can picture Janey's long hair, her dark eyes, her boundless energy. I can almost smell her. God, I love that woman, and to think we've been apart for so long. How stupid was I letting her go, but I guess we were young, foolish, and not ready. Now, though, I'm not going to let this chance pass me by. She deserves the best weekend ever. She'll really know how much I love her.

Come on now, don't panic. The walkway is different to the sections with cones. I can get down on all fours and feel my way back to the door.

Was there a handle on the inside? It had always been open

when I came in here. But there must be a handle, right? Behind one of the cones or something. There has to be. I can feel round for it when I get there.

Where was the guy locking up? Surely he should be coming? I can't see my watch, but it was close to home-time when I came in here.

Maybe Janey would realise where I was. She knew I was working here for the summer. She worked here last year, between her first and second years, before we went out. It was Janey who suggested the place, partly because of this amazing room. She said it felt really weird after a while, when you could start to hear the sounds of your own body. She loved her summer here. She spent some of the time playing a game with the security guards, first off lifting her pass with her hand obscuring most of it, then later when she'd managed to get a credit card – one of those Access ones – she noticed the green was quite similar to the passes, so she got in with that. Later on she just held up paper, or a hand, as she came through. She's like that, Janey – so confident when she wants to be.

Where's the damned door? It's so black, and my eyes are

starting to see things – shapes – that I know aren't there. Flying things buzzing about. I can hear some kind of buzzing. No, it's a whooshing sound. Is that me? Or am I imagining it. Where's the door?

My parents are away, so they won't be there to let her in. What will she do? She knows I'd be there. I'm never late. Never. She used to be late, so she probably won't even have arrived yet. I found that so frustrating when we first went out, but it'll be better this time. I'm calmer now, happier in myself. More confident.

OK, here's the wall. Is it the door? There's no obvious crack, but this has to be where the door would be, because I've followed the walkway. About handle-height, there are the usual cones. They do come off, so I can pull each one off in turn and feel… just the wall behind. No handle. There has to be one. Balls.

I shout again. Damn that stupid door, I need to get out of here. I'm not late. I've never been late for her. I can't be late – not for my chance to make this right, to get back with her. God, I love her.

This was going to be – no, it is going to be – the best weekend ever. Even better than the last time, when she popped down for a weekend, again when my folks were away. We went out to a nice restaurant and we had a lot to drink, and we went back and… oh, she is such a good kisser. We raided mum's gin cabinet, and then started making out on the sofa, and it was her first time too. It was a bit awkward at first, but she settled into it, and then I carried her upstairs. The romance of it all. She was tired, and a bit woozy by that stage, but she flopped onto bed and we had the best time ever. Even in here, trapped in this sodding room, I'm still smiling at the memory of it. More than just smiling.

Where's that handle? The cones come off, from near the floor, from higher up, from the sides – where's that damned handle? Come on, it's got to be…

YES!

A handle. Thank heaven for that. Turn, and I'm out of here.

It turns.

I pull. I push. The door doesn't budge.

But that's not possible, surely? It doesn't lock automatically, does it? People come in here to do experiments – it can't just swing shut and be locked?

Come on, breathe. Right, think. The tag is still there.

Someone will come. Someone has to come.

How much air is there in here? How long can a person survive in an airtight chamber?

Stop fucking breathing so much!

Shit shit shit.

Come on, Janey – realise where I am and come looking.

Someone, come looking!

Please?

Why now? After I've finally convinced her to come back, after all this time? I slump down with my back to the door. I want to hit something, to smash the door, to smash through the walls. Why now?

She'll think I'm late. I hate that. I hate that almost as much as being trapped in this stupid room. I'm never late. Not even by a minute. She'll laugh it off, though, like she always did when she was late, like when she couldn't decide what to wear for my friend's twenty-first. She kept changing clothes and changing clothes, and kept saying it was fine if we were there half an hour late, but I wanted to be there from the beginning. He was my friend. He'd said eight, so I wanted to be there at eight, and Janey kept changing her whole outfit. I kept telling her she looked great in anything, but that didn't seem to cut it, and when it got past eight and she still hadn't decided, I got so angry with her. Then she ended up deciding she felt ill and not coming. She did that a few times while we were going out, and it kept winding me up so much. I don't know if she realised how much until I properly lost my temper with her. I slapped her. I shouldn't have. I know that, but it just kept happening. We ended up not going out much – I guess it was right we split up, at least back then. So we could both get to know ourselves. I wish she were here now, opening that door. I'd leap into her arms so fast. Come on, someone.

It's taken weeks to persuade her to come back. Her mum said she didn't want to talk to me, but I knew that wasn't true. I knew deep down she felt the same for me, and I'm right. She's back. She's here if only I can get out of this stupid stupid room.

We finally spoke, and I reminded her of that night, of all the wine, and the kissing, and the bedroom. I told her how sexy it was. She was surprised I remembered at first, but it was our first time – of course I'd remember. Besides, I'd borrowed my dad's camcorder and took a tape of her lying there. Damn, she looked so hot. Hotter than anything I've seen on the internet. I told her that, and I guess that's when things really changed. She realised how much I loved her, and how beautiful I thought she was. That's when she finally melted and agreed to come down.

I can see her, lying on the bed in that video, right now. I can see her breathing, and her head rocking slightly. She's just sprawled back on the bed. God, how many times have I watched that, hoping she'd come back to me, and now I'm stuck here is this fucking room, which no one has checked, and how much air is there in here? Shit, someone, come back and check the room!

The tag was there when I came in. I know it. They have to come back and check all the tags when they lock up. They have to. I can picture it now. As I walked in, there it was:

hanging by the door. I walked in here, walked up the central walkway to replace a cone, and I was just leaning down. I can remember that moment, just before it went dark.

The weirdest thing was I thought I heard someone's voice, someone familiar, just for a second.

Good Call

I'd had an interview. And since this is before mobile phones or anything, I give our student house number, and stay in.

It's the end of an era. Dad had picked up my bulky stuff, so I'm reduced to living off takeaways and running dangerously low on knickers. My housemates had left, each in their own style. Gary snuck off without a word. Justin elaborately wished everyone well. Nicky looked ready to cry. Geordie and Frankie gave me overlong hugs. Now I'm alone in what had been drug-addled chaos. I walk round each room, seeing ghosts. A burnt ring on the carpet where we'd re-enacted the early scene from Alien with a cut-up watermelon and a metal bin – Justin had gone mental and screamed at us. The window where my boyfriend-of-the-time Jo had climbed up the drainpipe and got in to surprise me – nicely, I might add, not unwanted. I couldn't have ended up with Jo, though. Jo and Jacky? No.

The house seems huge. The claustrophobia of the last two years melts away. The phone rings.

I run downstairs. Hello?

Paula.

No, I haven't heard yet. I'll let you know.

I open the French windows in Frankie's room – the room that ended up as hers and Geordie's. Out there we'd nailed Justin's rabbit hot-water-bottle cover to a cross at Easter and called it the Easter bunny. We'd been drunk, if that's not obvious. He'd gone mental. Again.

The builder's yard behind the house had provided the bricks to make our barbeque, and a month back we'd had a final party. I got off with… oh shit, I can't remember. Good snogger, but it was never going to be more. Fantastic party though.

That's the phone.

Frankie.

No, I haven't heard yet.

Yes, I'm still here. Obviously.

Yes, I'm staying 'til… look, I don't want to be rude, but could I talk to you later?

Back outside the bricks bring back memories. Gary

managed to hide our kitchen table and chairs. His dad's a removal man, and he'd managed to fit them in the understair cupboard. We didn't even look there – it was way too small. He'd replaced it with a mound of bricks with pipes coming out. Wish I had a photo of it. Need I say how Justin reacted? He went mental.

    The phone.

    I almost trip over the frayed carpet.

    No, Dad, I haven't heard. Can I call you back?

    He hangs up slightly too quickly. Mum told him to call.

    I read.

    Phone again.

    Paula again.

    Yeah, come over. Wine? Good call. This is futile.

    Not many of us have made first interviews, let alone second, but it's still depressing to fail.

    Paula arrives, with her usual bottle of chilled Piesporter Michelsburg, which seems posh. I find two glasses, and we begin.

There is nothing on this planet like two people who enjoy each others' company simply realising that they're both embarked on one of mankind's noblest pursuits – that of getting absolutely wankered.

One bottle isn't enough, so I dig out a bottle of Thunderbird.

If you don't know, because you're young and haven't experienced Thunderbird, it's a very cheap wine. At least I think it was wine. Vaguely winey. Goes down a treat.

The phone rings.

Look, I'm tired of people calling, I'm getting drunk, just go away.

A pause.

A voice says my name.

A little bit of my brain kicks back to life. Oh good God it's them.

No, I shout. Hang on. I'll get her.

Footsteps away from the phone.

Deep breaths. Oxygen, girl, oxygen. The first hints of a headache threatening.

Footsteps leading back.

Posh voice. Hello? What the hell am I doing, trying a posh voice?

Yes, it is.

Really?

That's marvellous. Marvellous? I've never used the word marvellous before or since, but whether they realised my deception or not, the job's mine.

Shortlisted in "Writers' Forum" magazine.

Echo of the Storm

Dan couldn't see the curves of the bay through the driving rain. The storm was getting worse, and Jenni was out there. He hoped she would circle round and wait. She was experienced; she'd know what to do.

The rocks at the end of the bay disappeared into the waves. Dan caught sight of a bent-over old woman struggling along the coast road. No one should be out in this, he thought, least of all someone so frail. He watched her turn and climb up onto the rocks above the harbour. She drew herself up to her full height, and lifted her arms outwards as if willing the winds to take her.

She screamed, piercing the wind and rain. The noise made his bones hurt, like a knife scraping a china plate.

Without thinking Dan grabbed his cagoule and rushed out of the cottage, heading over to her. What on earth she was doing there, and what was wrong?

The scream was agony when it came again. He was

half way down the road, at the junction. To the left the potholed tarmac took you down to the harbour. To the right the muddy path took you out to the tourist-information-approved viewpoints. Even with his walking shoes on he didn't fancy the rocks ahead, but that's where the screaming woman was. Her arms were stretched out. The rain and winds seemed to be circling her, blowing her long skirt back and forth. He couldn't see how her shawl stayed on. The screaming grew louder, and Dan could barely hear the rain. The waves down on the shore burst up high into the sky.

In the distance Dan saw a ship, appearing out of the darkness. Jenni? No, it wasn't her small yacht, but something larger, something older-looking. A giant grey beast appearing from the distant sea, just about to turn and round the headland.

The woman's arms thrust down and forwards. The waves obeyed her, crashing in different directions, pushing the grey ship back out away from the island.

Through a lull in the rain Dan was able to make out the ship more clearly. Just one man, in a grey or green uniform, stood holding a rifle as he held onto the railing at the bow.

Behind the ship, thrown suddenly upwards by an unnatural wave, Dan saw Jenni's yacht, clear as anything, almost tossed into the sky before disappearing.

He screamed for her. The woman turned, her own scream turning into echoes as the sound of the wind returned.

Jenni held on with all her strength. She might be tied on, but that wasn't much comfort; she'd be smashed repeatedly against the boat if she relied on that cable in this storm. To be so close, but so tired. The winds had been rising all afternoon, but it had been something she could cope with, especially knowing a hot bath was waiting for her. This storm hadn't been forecast, and part of her grip on the rail now was paralysis. She had seen the island from further out, but now it was hidden. A wave threw her small boat up into the sky. She caught sight of the harbour, with its tiny array of lights, but something else in front. Another ship. She hadn't seen it before – where had it come from?

She stared, hanging on for dear life. The ship was too close, but surely it would have seen her. How could she have missed it? If she turned now she'd have a good chance of being blown away from the island, which would at least mean not crashing, but she was so tired.

The ship tried to make the turning into the bay. Jenni knew it was turning too soon. Surely it had to know about the rocks? They were clearly marked on the charts – there was even a wreck down there to make the point. A man appeared on the side of the deck – the only sign of life on board. Jenni became aware of a high-pitched scream in the distance.

The grey ship turned. Not much, but with the unmistakable grinding sound that meant it had run onto the rocks. The sound continued for so long, it had to be tearing a hole in the side. The man on the deck looked down at Jenni. He looked up into the sky, as if saying goodbye, and then leapt into the water.

Jenni knew there was no way he'd survive from out there. It might only be a few hundred metres, but there was no chance of swimming it. She grabbed her wheel and tried to turn herself around. She might be able to get closer. It meant getting closer to the rocks, but you can't just leave someone…

Dan heard the grinding sound too, and with it the old woman began her scream once more. For a second flashes of other figures appeared on the ship. The beast turned, and then began twisting in a way a ship would never do unless it was sinking.

Down by the harbour dim yellow lights appeared through the darkness, and as the old woman softened her scream, they joined in, giving the piercing sound some nightmarish harmony.

Dan saw Jenni's yacht again, this time turning towards the rocks. He shouted, uselessly. Why was she going towards the rocks? What was she thinking? She knew this harbour like the back of her hand. If she couldn't make it in, just head out to sea again and wait for calm.

"There won't be calm," shouted the woman. "There will never be calm again."

"What?" He was amazed how loud her voice was – stronger than his.

The chorus in the harbour grew louder, as more faint

lights appeared and disappeared again around the sinking grey hulk. As each light drifted under the water, a light on the harbour went out, until one by one they were all gone, and Dan turned back to the old woman.

"Any one of them could have made this harbour in their sleep, even in a storm."

"What?"

"And look. All of them. All gone!" She began her scream again.

Jenni could see the man in the water. He couldn't be more than seventeen or eighteen. He struggled in the waves in what looked like heavy clothing. He wasn't going to last long. She wasn't far away, but through the waves it was going to be hard to get any closer, especially with the rocks. Jenni grabbed her lifesaver with one hand and pulled her arm back, then swung, hoping it would get close enough.

The man saw the bright orange object flying at him, and made one more effort to kick himself up in the water. His hand grabbed the rope just behind the float, and he began pulling himself in.

Jenni turned the boat round, hoping now she could make some headway away from the rocks, assuming the man could hold on for at least a few seconds.

Her yacht turned and moved grudgingly, far enough that she felt safe enough to begin pulling him in. The weight of the rope was the only sign he was still there, until finally his face appeared through a wave, and she was close enough to lean down and offer him a hand.

It took way more effort than she expected to get him up enough to grab the railing himself. He was wearing an insanely heavy jacket, and heavy boots – it was amazing he'd managed to remain afloat at all.

The wind turned again, and the gust caught her abeam. The yacht tilted sideways, almost knocking the man off again, and with horror she realised she was mere metres from the rocks. She grabbed the man's hand, trying to keep him looking at her rather than turning. She knew he was about to be shipwrecked for the second time in a matter of moments.

"Where's she gone?" shouted Dan as he lost sight of Jenni again.

The woman turned her hands, the winds swirled round her, moving outwards until the eye of the storm included Dan.

"They're all gone. Any one of them, even my Bill, could have brought that ship in, even in their sleep. "

"Gone? Gone where?"

"Dead. All dead. We watched them die, and the women in the harbour all comforted each other, but they didn't even know about me and Bill. They left me out. They told me I was just being a foolish girl with a crush. They said Bill wasn't even a man, and I was too young. I told them about us, and they didn't believe me. I lost the baby, the last of him, and they didn't believe that either."

"Who's Bill?"

"Can't you understand? For years we had waited for news, for them to come home for good, fearing every time anyone got a telegram, and after all the shelling, all the trenches, they were a hundred yards from home. We saw them. We saw them sink. I saw Bill jump, trying to get away from the rocks, but he sank. He looked at me as he sank. I never got a chance to tell him about the baby."

Dan saw the yacht appear above a wave again, now close enough he could see Jenni on board. And someone else with her. They were way too close to the rocks now.

"Is that him?"

The old woman turned and looked down, eyes wide. Her hands moved once more and this time the wind calmed for a second, and then turned away from the rocks and towards the harbour. Jenni's little yacht flew up on a wave, almost over the rocks, before slipping back again and out into safer water.

The old woman turned and began running. Dan followed her.

Jenni let the man go and turned back to the wheel. The boat's little engine might not be able to save them, but she had to try. She pushed the throttle as far forward as it would go, willing the boat to get away, but the wind was too strong. She could almost hold it, but that wasn't enough any more.

Jenni felt a fear gripping her. She watched the rocks,

and felt a pain in her gut where she realised she'd made a mistake, but she couldn't have left him. That would be worse, surely, to get to the shore knowing she'd left a man to drown?

To be so close to home… She braced herself for the crunching that would mean the carbon fibre had been pierced, and the icy cold would take them. As she waited, she reached out and held the man's hand. It was freezing cold.

A wave lifted them suddenly, and Jenni drew in a deep breath, tempted to shut her eyes, but knowing she'd feel the crunch. The boat lurched backwards underneath them. Her feet lifted momentarily up off the deck, so much so that if she hadn't been holding the man's hand, or he hadn't been holding the rail, she might have been swept off.

The boat tilted, but no crunch came.

A wave crashed over them as they dropped back down, and Jenni could see the rocks. Slightly further away now. She held the man's hand even harder, not understanding how the wind could have shifted so suddenly. They must have flown almost over the rocks on that one wave, but somehow changed direction in the air. It made no sense.

Another wave crashed over the boat, then another, but each getting progressively smaller. She felt herself shaking all over, still stuck feeling she was about to drown.

She turned the little boat to the harbour.

The water flattened as the harbour walls surrounded them, and in a blur Jenni threw her rope out to a man. Dan. She tied the boat, and leapt onto the harbour and into his arms.

Dan held Jenni. Over her shoulder he saw the old woman stop a short distance away. She stooped down, bent over almost double, her full age becoming clear again.

She looked at her hands, horrified, and seemed to be about to turn.

The young man stepped ashore and walked up to her. "My love," he said. "Sorry I've been so long."

First published in "Romance" magazine. Also published in the Russian "Fables" anthology, volume 1.

Strangeness on a Train

"Why don't we get a man's perspective?"

I was on the edge of sleep, still trying to fight it off so I wouldn't miss my change at Reading, and her words didn't sink in until she spoke again.

"Oh, he's asleep."

I turned and looked at them: a stunningly bright-eyed peroxide blonde by the window, wearing a vest, a rose-with-thorns tattoo covering her nearside shoulder. Another girl, probably closer to my age, sat in the aisle seat. She had lovely black hair and dark eyes you could get lost in. I must have been tired or drunk not to notice either as I'd stumbled to my seat half an hour before. I'd been in Bristol, with its veritable cornucopia of fine drinking establishments. I had to spend a few seconds forcing them into focus.

"Sorry," said the dark-haired girl, glancing briefly back to the blonde with what looked like a flash of anger. "Didn't mean to wake you."

I realised there had also been some relief in her earlier "he's asleep" declaration, but it didn't process in my tired brain until I'd already answered their original question: "On what?"

"Sorry?"

"A man's perspective on what?"

The darker girl, who I noticed had a hint of Indian colouring about her, and was also very pretty, looked down. The blonde spoke up. "My friend Janni here," she said, smiling, "has been receiving naughty texts from a colleague. She's wondering what to do." Naughty. What a word to use. Her smile was evil, but it lit up her face. I stared into her piercing blue eyes for a little too long.

"I'm married," said Janni, as if to relieve the tension of my inability to put words together. "With a four-year-old son."

"Oh." I wasn't managing scintillating – that was for sure.

"But she's excited about him," added the blonde. "In a way she hasn't been for years. She wants to snog him."

Snog.

My first girlfriend had always called it snogging, and I

could still remember the joy I'd felt with her as we held each other and the world had melted away. My wife hated the word, and we'd never had that kind of wild abandon. You don't have it so much when you meet in your thirties rather than your teens.

I noticed the thumb on my left hand was pushing my wedding ring, pulling the finger so it wasn't so obvious. Realising that had happened made me feel instant guilt – it shouldn't be instinctive to hide being married, for heaven's sake, but there was more: I was remembering that first girlfriend, and noticed a look in the blonde's eyes that reminded me of her. I was imagining what holding her would feel like. What a proper snog with her would be like. As if I'd asked, her lips moved apart, just enough to see a hint of a tongue behind, licking the edge of her teeth.

I don't know what came over me. Well, I suppose I do. "If you're careful," I said, not knowing where I was going. "Surely falling into someone else's arms – proper snogging – feeling alive – surely that's a good thing?" Did I know what I was saying? Did the blonde know what I was saying? She certainly kept smiling as if she did, and narrowed her eyes and broadened her grin at the same time. Like I was prey. Willing prey.

"There you are!" she said, slapping Janni on the thigh.

"I don't know," said Janni, but now she too had a hint of a mischievous grin. "What if my husband finds out. I couldn't bear to lose him."

Without thinking I spoke again. "Be careful. Enjoy a moment of real passion, and then accept it's gone and go back to your safe life." I looked at Janni, and saw her surprise at how I'd said it, how I'd felt it, and then I looked beyond her. To the blonde, who was pointedly grinning, and I felt butterflies – no, I felt sick. I felt terrified and thrilled, and resentful suddenly that Janni was there.

And more than any of these, I felt alive. I wasn't tired. My heart was racing.

"I don't know," said Janni again. "I do get this feeling when I'm around him, and I… I don't know."

"Why do you think one person is always supposed to be with just one other anyway?" asked the blonde again. "We're so messed up that way. Life is for living." She looked like she lived by that rule. It flashed through her eyes, and definitely in those oh-so-kissable lips.

"I suppose."

"He knows, I presume," I asked.

"Who? Knows what?"

"Your 'naughty' friend. He knows you're married?"

"Oh yes."

"And he just wants some fun?"

"Yes."

"So."

"So, would you?" she asked, emphasising that now the question was about me.

Blimey. At that moment, right then, I would, yes. I'd got hard with just the thought of it, let alone actually doing anything. Let alone the beautiful blonde making a move towards me. A kiss, stolen out of life, a moment of true abandon…

WE ARE NOW APPROACHING READING.

Janni stood up and grabbed a bag from the rack.

"What are you going to do?" asked the blonde.

Janni smiled, looking so beautiful suddenly. "I don't know. But this has been… It's been something. I might." She grinned again, and walked up the corridor, looking so much taller than I expected, looking so happy. Looking… loved?

It was my stop too. Miss it and I would have to get a cab back from London. Sixty, seventy quid.

But I didn't get up.

I looked over at the blonde's face, and she smiled back, as if waiting for me to say something, or possibly waiting for me to come over and fall into her arms. To kiss her. To snog her, like I hadn't snogged anyone for years. To feel alive again, after so many years of being… well, if not sensible, at least vaguely responsible.

I was so turned on I thought she had to notice, but she didn't look down. In a moment I'd gone from moving next to her, to kissing her beautiful young lips, to going home with her. I was waking up the next morning next to her, having spent the night with someone so alive, so passionate, so full of energy I could just live off that for years to come. It would be everything I'd ever fantasised about, from the prison of a beautiful loving family.

    I shut my eyes for a second, feeling the train slowing to a halt. I opened them to see her sidle slightly towards the empty seat, and then I stood up.

    "Sorry," I said, abruptly. It hurt to say it. It felt like I'd punched myself.

    "My new friends? Both going at once?"

    I didn't answer. How could I answer? How could I say another word without turning round and falling into her arms, into her lips, into those eyes?

    I stumbled along the corridor. Janni was surprised to see me as we stood by the door waiting for it to activate. She leaned slightly and said "Well, that was a rather liberating conversion." She was smiling so hard her cheeks had big dimples in them.

    I just nodded.

    We stepped down out of the carriage, and I took a few steps away before looking back at the carriage window.

The blonde didn't turn. I heard Janni walking off, and I stopped and waited until the train moved, but the blonde never turned. She looked forward, perhaps asleep, perhaps just daydreaming.

The train pulled out of the station. I saw a fleck of the blonde hair, but nothing of those eyes. Nothing of those lips.

I turned and saw Janni, still looking up at the sign boards. She began to walk towards one of the distant platforms, until I shouted "Wait!"

Janni turned, and waited.

I ran over to her. "Look," I said. "I realise this is none of my business, but that conversation…" It felt stupid to be saying this. It wasn't my business, but I felt responsible, somehow. Plus arguing this might make my own decision seem something other than throwing away a potential moment of joy.

Janni grinned again. "Liberating." She looked so wistful.

I shook my head. "I think it was, but I think that's as good as it gets. Do you love your husband?"

"Of course."

"Then go back to him, and just remember that moment of fantasising."

"Is that what you'd do?"

"It's what I am doing."

Janni looked back to where the train had been. "Avril?"

"If that's her name, yes. For a moment there, I would have risked it all for her."

"But not now?"

"No. Not now."

Janni looked back towards where the train had been, thoughtfully. "I need to…" She shook her head and turned to the platform she'd been heading towards.

"Yeah. OK. Anyway, sorry if I…"

She smiled again, a sadder smile this time. "No, I had a moment. A moment of escape."

I turned to look for my connecting train, feeling smaller and lesser than I had been. Tiredness coming back, maybe.

I sat on the platform, and watched, unthinking, as my

short train pulled in. I sat on it, feeling dead inside. There was no one else in the carriage – possibly not even on the train. No beautiful blonde, with lips to die for. Just a few free newspapers sat folded on seats. Only as I left the train at my station and climbed the hill, to my wife and fast-asleep children, did I start feeling something else. Something which kept me going during the climb.

Perhaps escape had been the right word.

Highly commended by Southport Writers' Circle and published on their website.

Stranger Stranger

Where'd I put my damned ticket? If only I could stick this flashing bloody cutlass somewhere I'd be more organised. That or if I wasn't so tired. We'd be home by now if Fin hadn't forgotten his sweets, or if I was hard-hearted enough just to tell him he'd lost them so tough luck, or if I wasn't so skint that even three quid for sweets is too much. Truth is we don't have enough money to go out at all, but his Mum had promised him Peter Pan, so it had to be Peter Pan, every year, and Wimbledon had been the closest place doing it.

Of course the tickets are in the pocket I looked in first. Always are, but hid from me first time. I hand one to Fin, and then quickly swap when I see mine says "child" on it. He's ahead of me. I adjust his drink in one of my overstuffed pockets to check it isn't about to fall out. There are nuts and raisins in the other – snacks which we'll have because it's going to be a late supper, especially if we miss the five-past train. Come on, people – stop dawdling.

I get buffeted sideways by a fat woman pushing through. Oh come on – this would be quicker if we all just queued. What's happening to this country if we can't queue?

Fin's just to the right now. He's going through the barrier in a second, so I'd best get through this one. Another man tries to push in front of me, but I hold my place this time, pushing him back a little. He gives me a nasty look as I slip my ticket into the barrier and get through. He pushes me again when he emerges from the barrier behind me, and I drop the cutlass.

Leaning down to pick it up I lose sight of Fin for a second. I spot him still behind the barrier, as if he too has been pushed out of his place. I must teach him to be more forceful with queueing. One time we were at a pizza demonstration and they offered the chance for children to make their own pizzas. Fin was near the front, right next to where the queue began to form, but as he tried to get to the back of the queue it grew as fast as he moved. He didn't get to make pizza at all – they ran out of time. He remembers that sometimes and wants to go back, but we can't afford it anymore. He doesn't understand why, but knows it's something about Mum.

Hang on – I can't see him.

Where's he gone?

I look around, getting hit by another overburdened Christmas shopper, but I can't see him.

"Daddy!"

My parental instinct kicks in. Even with all the noise, a parent knows their own child, and knows when they're in trouble. He was over there somewhere, way back behind the barriers. I jump to see better, and catch a glimpse of him. Some woman with blonde hair and a dark jacket is pulling him, but he saw me for a second. Oh my God. My brain turns into a machine.

I look at the entry barriers, but the queue there is way too long. I run to the disabled gate, but there's a wheelchair coming through. I pull the chair through so it's out of my way, and the man who was helping shouts at me. He pushes me back and the gate closes behind him. He says something about me being a bigot.

The barriers aren't all that high, so I grab onto a broken

one and leap up. The cutlass falls once again. I leave it lying on the ground, flashing pink and green.

Several people shout at me, but this time I don't care how hard I push them away. Fin's over there, being led to the other exit.

He hasn't shouted again. Why not?

Shout boy, shout!

A man grabs me, and I shake my arm and try to get free, but he's strong.

I look at him - he's a ticket guard. I shout, as quick as I can: "My son's over there. He's been taken!"

"Look, sir, you can't just jump the barriers."

"Do you understand what I'm saying?" I'm shouting into his face now. I sense my right hand forming into a fist. I've only got seconds. It doesn't matter how polite I ought to be.

"Please calm down, sir."

My right hand draws back, and then gets stuck. Someone else has grabbed it. I turn, and see another guard.

"Right, come with us," says the second man.

"Fin!" I shout, and struggle to get away. They don't let go. Why don't they understand? They have to let me go.

Fin!

* * *

"Where'd I put my damned ticket?"

I always put it in my waistcoat pocket, but it isn't there. I'm too old to be coming into London, especially near Christmas, but I wanted that tea Sarah always liked so much. It's stupid, I know. I'll be on my own, but I still want to do everything the way she used to, making everything just so. It feels important at Christmas. Jake's down in New Zealand with his family. He asked me to come, but it's too far to travel. I'm getting too old.

I hear someone mutter a swear word and push me. I'm standing at the top of the stairs, in the way. Still can't find that ticket.

I step sideways to get out of the throng of people. So many people. I don't like being bumped around – I don't want to have another fall.

It's not in my jacket pocket either. Where the devil is it?

Try the waistcoat pocket again. Of course it's there. How didn't I find it first time?

There's so much noise.

A boy just ahead of me shouts "Daddy". He's being dragged along by his mother.

Odd that he should turn and shout that, though. His mother smacks him round the side of the head. You're not supposed to do that nowadays, although no one thought twice about it when I was young. There was one time I couldn't hear anything in one ear for days after being hit by my form master. I'm a bit deaf in that ear now, come to think of it.

The boy looks properly shocked, like he hasn't been smacked before. He was really trying to get away for a second there.

His mother looks furious. She's probably tired too. It's hard if you have to drag a child along shopping, especially with all these people.

There's something odd in the way he shouted.

I don't entirely understand why, but it feels necessary to do something. I lean out and grab the mother's arm.

"Excuse me, but you shouldn't hit a child like that."

The boy looks up at me. It looks like he's about to speak. His mother grabs his shoulders. It looks like it's hurting. "What's it got to do with you?"

"He doesn't look very happy."

"Staring at boys, are you? Fucking paedo."

She says the word paedo really loud, and people start staring.

"Let go of my fucking arm," she adds.

There another loud shout down by the barriers. The boy looks sideways, and then twists round. He's still being held firmly, but puts his hands together and throws his arms up between his mother's in what looks like a martial-arts move. She loses her grip for a second, and the boy runs.

His mother grabs at him, yanking her arm free of my grip, bashing my arm in the process. That's going to bruise. Everything does, nowadays.

She looks over at where the boy has gone, and I'd have expected her to run after him, but she looks scared, and heads the other way.

I start after the boy, wondering if he'll need some help, hoping no one else will shout anything abusive.

The crowd is dense, and I can only see glimpses of the boy's blond hair, and hear him shout again: "Daddy".

*   *   *

I'm still struggling with the guards when I hear him. "Daddy."

I take one deep breath and stop moving. "That's my son." I'm trying to sound calm.

"Where?"

"That shout. He's looking for me. Fin!" I shout as loud as I can, and people turn to stare. I don't care. "FIN!"

There's a shout back. He's close.

He runs through a gap between surprised shoppers. He leaps up at me. The guards are so shocked they let go. I'm knocked back against a barrier by this beautiful boy, heavier than I can comfortably carry any more, throwing himself up at me.

I hold him, feeling his trembling heart against my chest even through his thick jacket. It's the most wonderful cuddle I've ever had.

I apologise to the guards for what I did, and explain. There's time and calm now Fin's back. They accept my apology. An old man comes over, and Fin manages "woman", "dragged me away", "that man stopped her" which gives us enough of an idea what happened. The guards' interest perk up again, and they ask him to come with them to make a statement and check security footage.

He sounds sad as he says he doesn't have anywhere he needs to be. They want us to come too. Fin accepts being put on the ground, but he's holding my hand so tight it hurts. I don't mind, and I don't ask him to loosen it. I'm probably hurting his hand too. He's slightly ahead of me so I can watch him. The world seems hazy outside of the two of us. Nothing else matters. Nothing else really exists. It's oddly quiet.

We get taken to a small office with dozens of screens. The old man describes a forty-something slightly overweight blonde woman in a black jacket and blue jeans, and the guards start looking all over the screens, pressing buttons to make the pictures flash back and forth.

Fin looks over and shouts. "There! That's her!"

The old man nods. "Looks like her."

There's whispering into walkie-talkies, and only seconds later we see, on the screen, two policemen walk up to the woman and lead her away.

There is taking of names and addresses, including an exchange with the old man. I mutter something about wanting to thank him. But nothing is real except that I have Fin next to me. I don't feel anger or hatred. Somewhere deep down I feel I should, but it's not there. Just relief.

The old man becomes William, and spends Christmas with us, even conjuring Fin a Christmas present from somewhere. Pulling three crackers seems a lot more festive than two.

He apologises that he didn't manage to find anything for me. He doesn't realise he already gave me the best present I've ever had.

First published in "Every Day Fiction" fiction website.

Survivor Guilt

I watched from the wall as they began arriving. First in ones and twos, then larger groups of desolate soldiers trudging towards the city. There was no doubting what this meant: the capital had fallen. The walls which had held for four-hundred years were breached.

The horde would follow.

Behind me I could see the dusty road that led to the border. Already it was jammed with carts slipping away. We had been ordered to search anyone trying to leave, ensuring they didn't take food or weapons. How were they meant to reach safety without food or weapons? How were they meant to reach it at all? Was there anywhere safe?

We had also been given orders to stand here, no matter what the cost, if only to give our countrymen time.

When my watch ended I walked home past the infirmary. I lingered by the door, listening for a few minutes.

"There were too many of them."

"It was carnage. Only a small number of us…"

"…burnt everything…"

"…harried us all the way…"

"…it's all gone…"

"…the stench. You can't imagine…"

"On the last day we broke out. We abandoned them all. We don't deserve to live." That last voice was so tragic. He sounded like he wanted only the relief of death. I leant in through the door. There was nothing physically wrong with him. He stared wide-eyed as he gripped another man's shoulders. "We made a mistake leaving them. I won't make that mistake again. God will see that I stand here. And die if He wills it." These were the survivors, and they would stand with us.

At home my son greeted me by leaping up. As if nothing was wrong. I looked at my wife. Her face showed nothing, but her eyes were sad. I said, "You have to go."

"Without you?"

"We've been through this, my love. I cannot leave.

For his sake, go."

She looked angry. It was unfair, I knew, but it might save their lives.

"You could…" she began, but I shook my head. I had taken the oath. There was no choice now.

"When?" she asked.

"Immediately. The horde cannot be more than a few days from here. If they surround the city, it will be too late."

She burst into tears. Our son ran over and hugged her, not understanding what was going on. He was a good boy. I would miss him. I would miss her. Not for long, at least – that was a comfort.

I needed to do something. "I will pack what you need."

"Where will we go?"

"As far as you can."

"I don't speak other languages."

"You will learn."

"I don't want…" I stepped forward and held her, and my son. I knew. But there was no choice.

The gate was closed when we arrived. I begged the captain, persuading him with now-pointless money. He took it all. Through the small door I could see a few distant carts. "Hurry," I said. "Catch up with them and you will be safer. A group of survivors is providing escort."

She tried to speak, but couldn't. They flung themselves at me. I pushed my wife and son away.

"Take care of him for me. Good luck."

I turned. It would only get harder the longer it took. The captain closed the gate, and her sobs were cut short. I hoped she wouldn't linger, but there was nothing I could do now. I had to get some rest before the battle began.

The survivors were scattered amongst us, filling our ranks. Seeing the numbers on the walls gave me brief hope, until I remembered who we were fighting. No walls could withstand the horde. No army could stop them. Sometimes no one survived – sometimes a few lived to tell the tale. My heart sank as a cold wind gusted round the city.

"The Baron has given orders," said a man near me, a

survivor. "No inch of the wall is to be surrendered. He will make a final stand in the keep. We must not leave our posts."

Of course we wouldn't. The walls looked strong. There was still no sign of any army. That gave me hope. Maybe there had been a miracle? At least my family would be long-gone before the horde reached us.

A horn blew, and there was commotion by the back gate. Surely my wife would not have returned?

Please God.

The word spread rapidly. An ambush. The survivors described their battle. They had been driven back, separated from the women and children. When a chance came to return, the slaughter was complete. With nothing to fight for, the survivors rode back for the city.

My heart was ice. I had only one task to accomplish now. To avenge them. To drag as many of the horde to hell as I could, to make them pay for what they had taken. My death now meant nothing.

I heard the horn sound three times. It was the sound of an attack, but still no army. A man to my right screamed. And one to my left.

    I saw a survivor thrust his sword through one of our soldiers and push him off the wall. The other side, the same. All along the walls, men were falling. I drew my sword to face the survivor in front of me. I recognised him from the infirmary, but his face was different now. He stared into my eyes, grinning. I raised my sword, parried his blow and responded as swiftly as I could. He crumpled, clutching his chest. I turned to face another, blocking a blow to my head. I prepared to counter, but felt the steel run me through from behind, and then a boot, and then merciful blackness, swallowing up the betrayal.

The Girl Of Our Dreams

It began slowly, one night when I was just nodding off. I assumed it was a dream – one of those dreams where you're half-awake and it could just about be real. I was standing inside the door of a hotel room, with a bathroom door to my left and the main bedroom ahead. The floor was tiled beneath my feet, but I couldn't feel it. I imagined it must be cold.

I'd been standing there for a few minutes, hearing distant sounds of a shower running. The sound stopped almost as soon as I became aware of it. The door opened, and wet footprints appeared on the tiles. Each toe produced its own tiny print as the footsteps headed away towards the carpeted area next to the bed.

That was all I saw the first time. Just footsteps.

I woke up, and thought nothing of it until the next night.

That night I was standing inside the door again, and the same happened. The same noise, the same footsteps, but this time there was a faint towel hanging in the air. I could still see the floor through it, but it was obviously wrapped round an invisible woman's body – it was too high to be round a man's waist. She was tall, for a woman, but still a few inches shorter than me.

Again I awoke, and again thought no more of it until the next night, a Tuesday, when the same thing began again, only this time the towel was more distinct and the woman within was a ghostly presence. She had long dark hair as she walked away from me. I didn't seem to be able to move. I could hear her this time, as she was muttering to herself – not quite distinct enough to make out, but it sounded like she was practicing some kind of talk. She paused, as if for effect, as if an audience was going to appreciate some point.

When I woke this time I felt odd, as if I'd been intruding, although I hadn't intended to. It did haunt me during the day though, and I was strangely keen to get to bed that night, wondering if this odd dream would recur.

No sooner had I laid my head on the pillow than I was back in the hotel room, except this time something was different. I could feel the tiles under my feet. I tried taking a step. I moved. Again the sound of the shower stopped, and this time the woman who walked out was quite clear. She had the towel wrapped around her, covering from her chest to a short way down her thighs. Her hair was wet and stuck to one shoulder.

She walked round the corner towards the bed, and I followed. She dropped the towel and began getting dressed facing away from me. After getting on knickers and jeans she turned round. She gasped as she saw me, her dark eyes wide open. She said something, but I couldn't hear what it was – just a muffled sound from a distance. She looked past me, seeing the closed door behind, and said something else. She recoiled, uncertain for a moment, but then stepped forward and put a hand out to me. It passed through, making a tingling sensation like when you've slept on your arm and it goes dead.

She stood in front of me, still topless, and I stared into her eyes. I lifted my arms, and touched her shoulders. She shivered, put her hand out again, and again it went through me.

I stroked her arm, and she flicked her head back as if it tickled.

She spoke again, but I still couldn't hear it. I tried to

speak, but my own voice was inaudible, even to me.

She sat down, and I sat down next to her and stroked her hair, then ran a hand down her back. She straightened up and shut her eyes, twitching slightly. Again she put a hand through me, and then seemed to shout something. I moved my hand, like I would with a woman who actually existed, up and down her back, which elicited the same reaction as before. I ran the other down one shoulder and across her chest, cupping one of her breasts briefly. She fell back onto the bed at this touch, lying sideways across it. She seemed out of breath.

I lay down next to her, gently caressing her front as she lay there. She looked up at me, still trying to speak, still inaudible, shaking her head. She pulled back for a moment, but then stopped and let me continue, or at least made no move to get away. She shut her eyes and seemed to be quivering, and eventually she reached down and unfastened her jeans and pushed them down. I ran my fingers further down, and her reaction to that was obvious. It took very little time before even in her silence I knew what she was feeling.

She opened her eyes, looking so fresh and young, so

happy, but when she stared at me her expression changed again to confusion. She spoke, but the sound was even more distant than before, and I felt it receding even further as I watched her lying naked on the bed, breathing heavily.

The scene faded into nothing, and she was gone. I lay awake in bed, staring up at the ceiling.

It had been so vivid, so lifelike. She was the most beautiful woman I'd ever seen, without question. Her dark hair, her eyes that were so alive, so filled with... filled with intellect. There was no other way to say it. She had seemed that way when I first saw her, practicing something, and she was still that way when I'd looked down at her – she had eyes which analysed, which knew, which could pierce your soul.

Her face stayed with me, and I was unable to concentrate on anything all day.

That night – Thursday – I couldn't even watch a comedy on TV during the evening. Every moment her beautiful face, her beautiful hair, her amazing body, those eyes, and the mind behind it all, they returned to me every time I blinked.

I went to bed early and laid down, shutting my eyes, but not getting to sleep tonight.

It took until midnight before I actually fell asleep, but when I did I was immediately back in that room. This time the scene was different. She was sat on the bed, and I could move so much more freely. I stepped into the bedroom area, and she looked up and smiled. She got up and looked past me to the door. I turned and saw she'd put the chain on. She traced a finger down the line of my shoulder, and only then did I notice I was wearing my pyjamas. Her finger went slightly into my arm, and made that fuzzy feeling again, but she didn't go through me so much - she was either now able to feel me or just working off sight.

She was still wearing work clothes – a very formal but elegant skirt and white top, with a light grey styled jacket. I held her in my arms, holding her waist and pulling her towards me, and as her face came closer I kissed her on the lips. She didn't respond with a kiss, but certainly felt it, shutting her eyes, opening her mouth, perhaps letting whatever feeling she had wash over her.

Again she tried to speak to me, but again the sound was muffled and distant. She seemed to realise that I couldn't hear her, so she gave up. She stood in front of me as I ran my fingers up and down her back, and then began undressing her, first slipping her jacket off her shoulders and then lifting up her tight-fitting top. She raised her arms to help me, and as her top fell I stroked down her arms to her breasts again, this time holding both. She stared into my eyes, awash with confusion.

She mouthed at me, and I definitely made out the words this time. Who are you?

I answered without thinking. I don't know.

Whether she understood or not I couldn't say, but I was lost now, and reached down and unfastened her skirt, which dropped to the floor. I pushed down her knickers, and she lay back on the bed. This time, though, aware of my own clothes, I removed those too, and lay on top of her and made love to her slowly.

Even as I came I felt the scene disappearing, and this time screamed out, wondering why it had to end. I looked into her eyes as she faded, and she gazed back with such a look of love as I had never seen before. Such a complete abandonment. Her fringe had fallen backwards, her hair was splayed out on the bed behind her. I took a last glance at her naked body lying so comfortably on the bed as she faded from view. If I could have closed my eyes at one instant and never seen another sight, that would have been the moment. Such beauty. Such love for me. Such joy. It actually hurt.

Friday was even worse. Colleagues suggested the pub, but I couldn't deal with that. I wanted to spend all day with my eyes shut, trying to keep every tiny detail of her perfect face and body in my mind all the time, waiting for the evening, waiting for my next dream.

I was lost in my own head, and couldn't think of anything else. I shouldn't even have gone in to work, and frankly shouldn't have been driving.

The evening ticked past so slowly it was agonising, and it was all I could do to leave the bottle of whisky untouched.

When the time finally came I went to bed, shutting my eyes and imagining her standing in front of me again, imagining her face looking at me, contented and relaxed.

My eyes were heavy, but I couldn't get to sleep at the normal time. It became a vicious cycle as I began getting frustrated with myself for not sleeping. I turned the radio on, which normally helped, and listened to a few minutes of the news before the tiredness finally overcame me.

But there was no dream. No hotel room.

I woke up when the radio switched off, and immediately turned it back on for another hour, trying to will myself back to that hotel room. Trying to find her again.

The night had little sleep in it, and no dreams. No woman.

Saturday morning dawned, and I was both exhausted and devastated.

The next night was the same.

Monday morning found me staring into a mirror looking at the dishevelled face in front of me, unwashed for two days and with probably less than three hours sleep over the whole weekend. Her face was fading from my mind with every imagining.

I took Monday off, ringing in and not having to fake

how bad I felt. This time the whisky did come out, and by the middle of the afternoon I was finally asleep, or at least comatose on the living room sofa.

I woke up in the middle of the night and went upstairs, a faint hope within me, but it remained unfulfilled. I slept through to morning, but whatever dreams I had were forgotten in the alcoholic haze.

On Wednesday I managed to wash and shave and went to the office, still a danger to other drivers, but at least able to do a little bit of work.

As the days passed her face appeared less and less in my imaginings, and I recovered enough to function normally in society again, ashamed of how my own dream had affected me.

A couple of months later I was offered the chance to go on a business trip to Jerusalem, which while being a dull conference, was at least a change of scenery, so I jumped at the chance. I'd never been there, and hoped I'd at least get a little look around the Old City.

I arrived in the hotel already tired, but it felt strange as I checked in. I couldn't put my finger on what it was, but the décor seemed familiar.

When I opened my door it hit me right away.

The bathroom was on the left. The tiled area beneath my feet. The bedroom ahead. Even the chain on the door was the same.

Was it just a similar room? Hotels are alike, after all, but I felt all shivery and sick looking round. The bed was identical, and for a second I felt I could remember the girl in my dreams lying there, looking up at me.

I sat on the side of the bed and looked around the room, gasping for breath. I had been tired, but that feeling was gone now. I needed water. I needed a drink.

I walked into the bathroom, and saw the shower and towels. Of course there would be a shower and towels. Why wouldn't there be?

I poured a small glass of water and then decided to go to the bar to calm my nerves.

Downstairs the barman looked surprised that I didn't want ice in my Chivas Regal – the best whisky they had – and was even more surprised when I needed a second within minutes. I nibbled on the small Bombay-mix type snacks they provided, and sat staring off into the distance. Behind me a load of Americans visiting the Holy Land came and went, chattering excitedly about walking "where Jesus had walked".

After a third whisky I started feeling more relaxed, more comfortable. I knew all about deja-vu, and I hadn't written down my dream or anything – I could just be overlaying a vague memory with what I was seeing now. It made more sense that way, and when I finished the drink I decided I'd just been imagining things, and went back upstairs, now back to feeling exhausted.

I got undressed, brushed my teeth, and went to lie down in bed, feeling a little troubled again, but not too much.

As I closed my eyes I felt something – something cold.

I opened them again, and there was something there. I knew before I got up to look.

She was standing there, just round the corner, just inside the door.

Faint at first, but slowly becoming more visible, the girl

from my dream was standing there in a nightie, her hair as beautiful as I remembered, hanging down with a few strands just in front of her shoulders, framing her pale face. Her eyes looked fearful for a moment, until she saw me. She walked towards me, and touched my shoulders. Her hands didn't go through any more.

I reached out to her, and this time it was she who was ethereal. My hand slipped inside her shoulder and through her arm, not feeling anything. I withdrew my hand again, and felt the tingle as she put a hand on the side of my neck.

She reached forwards again, and kissed me.

I almost collapsed. It was an incredible feeling, like every tingly massage, every electric shock, every feeling I'd ever had all rolled into one.

I put my hand out, hoping to feel her, trying to hold her hand, trying to stroke her back. She seemed to understand, and she followed me back to the bed and sat down astride me, and kissed me again.

My body exploded in sensations and I collapsed backwards.

She caressed me for a while, and I was lost, shutting my eyes and letting it wash over me.

When she stopped I opened my eyes and saw her mouthing something to me. She lay down, supporting herself on one elbow, looking into my eyes. Who are you?

I tried to mouth back, but she began fading away.

I reached out, and wanted to grab her, to keep her, but she disappeared.

The first day of the conference was dull anyway, but in my state I could barely take anything in. I listened and tried to take notes, but couldn't concentrate.

When the evening finally came I went out to a restaurant to try to think, but nothing made sense. I drank wine, I ate the food, but it had no taste to me. The world seemed apart, out of focus.

It only came together when I got back to the hotel room and sat down on the bed.

It was a matter of moments before I felt the cold.

I stepped round the corner, but this time she was standing there in full-length pyjamas, and didn't look at all happy to see me.

She shook her head.

I shrugged and tried to ask what was wrong. She couldn't hear me. I stepped forward again, but this time she stepped back, back to the door.

Why? I tried to ask. What's wrong?

She looked around, and tried to pull the handle of the door, but without success. She backed into the corner, and I realised that moving forward was making her more afraid. I stepped back towards the end of the bed and sat down.

She took a couple of steps forward so she could see me clearly, but made no move to come to the bed this time. She stood, as if waiting.

I opened my arms, asking for a hug, maybe. Something to feel calm again, but she stayed away.

She shook her head.

She didn't want to be here.

I didn't understand it at first, but I'd been so consumed with what had happened. It suddenly hit me. This girl was real. She wasn't just my dream. And this way round – her appearing when I was awake – that made it different. But she must have known that already? Why had she changed?

I tried again to mouth a question to her, but she faded away. I instinctively lunged forward, just to hold her hand for a second, and my hand just reached, and passed through hers before she vanished.

The next day's conference was useless to me, and it became obvious to my hosts that I wasn't paying attention, which wouldn't go well when I returned home, but I just couldn't focus.

My head was spinning, but differently now. When I returned to the hotel I sat in the bar and had a whisky again, thinking for a little while, running things through in my head.

I remembered her face, looking scared at me, and while I longed for her touch once more, I knew it wasn't going to happen. All I could do was trap her again and frighten her. I wanted to see her once more to say goodbye, but if I did – would I keep the little resolve I had?

Instead when I finished my whisky I went to reception and asked if there was a different room – maybe a smaller one.

The receptionist looked surprised, but checked and told me there was indeed another room, much higher in the hotel.

I went back and packed quickly, ready to move to the new room. I went as fast as I could, hoping I'd get finished before that cold feeling returned, and when I got my bag out to the corridor and shut the door behind me I felt enormous relief. The click of the door felt so final.

At least as I lay in my new room I didn't feel anything, just an emptiness.

I realised I couldn't picture her face any more, nor her beautiful hair and fringe. Just the vaguest concept of how lovely she'd been.

As I lay down to sleep I found myself crying.

The next day I managed to pay attention, which might have made up a little for before, but I felt so low it didn't matter. The boredom didn't matter. I tried to pay attention just for something to be in my head.

My final evening in Jerusalem involved a short walk round the Old City, but again it didn't register. The buildings were just bricks. Even the Western Wall was just big bricks with people praying in front of it. Nothing mattered. I walked past the sign explaining that the Jews believed this was the site of the Divine Presence, but there was nothing divine here for me.

The conference done, I headed back home to a dull job, a dull flat, and a total void. Her face wasn't with me any more, but I could still recall that first image of her walking away from me dressed in her towel, hair beautifully hanging over her shoulders. Every time I thought of it I felt a pain in my gut. She'd been terrified. It still made me sad, and between drinks I found myself wondering whether I could have communicated with her somehow – whether we could have broken that barrier.

Weeks passed meaninglessly, until work inexplicably decided to send me off again, this time to San Francisco. I arrived at Heathrow, the world continuing to be a blur around me as it had been for as long as I could now remember. I headed for the bar to drown the feeling, and ordered a whisky.

As I took a sip I saw her on the other side of the bar. She was sitting at a table reading a book. I stared for a while, watching until she turned sideways and her face came back to me. The rest of the world faded away with only her in existence, framed as if by a tunnel. I wanted to go to her, to reach out and touch her, to stroke her shoulder and flick her hair off it and hold her neck, to kiss her, to…

I took another sip.

She was real.

The world snapped back into view, and a joy flooded into me. An unadulterated joy, almost more than I could bear. I heard my own laughter, and felt people turning round to see me.

She was real.

She was sitting there.

In my waking world.

Her scared face came back to me, and I realised how terrifying it would be if I just appeared and sat down, trying to talk to her. After all, I'd seen her naked, touched her body, loved her, but never even met her.

I got out a business card and took a deep breath.

I walked over, circling round a little so I didn't just

appear right in front of her.

I waited a little way away until she had a chance to look up, and her face, stunningly beautiful, showed a whole range of emotions. First surprise, then a flash of affection, a moment of fear again, and then back to a forced calm.

On the way over I'd thought about what to say. It wasn't up to me now, but I wanted to make my feelings clear. I'd planned so much more, but all I managed to come out with was "I'm so glad you're real." It was all I could say. I placed my business card on the table, which had my mobile number and email on it. It was enough if she wanted to talk. Or anything else for that matter.

She smiled, but I couldn't stay and make it anything other than terrifying. I smiled back, and walked back to my whisky. I didn't finish it – I was too busy grinning. I felt her turn to look at me, but I didn't want to stare, so I settled up and walked out of the bar.

She was real.

The world seemed young.

I don't honestly know if I want her to call – I think I do, at least if she wants to – but I do have to remember that I don't actually know her.

Either way it goes, the world is now good. She is real.

The Texture Of The Trees

My authorisation came through, just as I was beginning to hope it wouldn't. I knew this was my last chance. Theirs, too.

I hated going back to Prime. You never felt welcome any more. It wasn't just the permit – it was the reduced clock all outsiders got, reduced relative to how far away they were from Prime.

No one voluntarily gave up real estate on Prime – at least not since I had. Only Zade even remembered we were once a happy community. When I first knew Prime it had been a wild frontier, creating something beautiful from nothing. It was Zade's say-so that gave me this chance to visit. The other entrants with me would be an army of paid servants helping to build the magnificent structures demanded by the Primates (that was my name for them, which unsurprisingly had never caught on). You can't even get there from most servers now, so protected were the few remaining portals. Some had been removed because they sat too close to First Site, and none of the Primates wanted people arriving close to that. Plus they hadn't just had their own portals removed - they had made sure the other servers were broken up into small clusters so they could only communicate through Prime, to avoid conspiracies. That was the selfish half of my motivation.

I lived way out in the fringe, on a largely unheard-of server, which might have shocked the other Primates, but most didn't even know who I was. They'd changed their nomenclature based on proximity to the First Site, the location of the first small shack built when the place was a game. Each Primate had a set of coordinates, indicating which part of their building-work managed to spike closest to that location. Had I stayed, I'd have been around fifth in the pecking order, but that would have depended on me keeping vigilant about other buildings spiking through mine. That was one of the jobs of the servant army – to patrol the walls of each property, making sure nothing got moved. Once moved the change would become permanent if it wasn't spotted by the time the change log rotated. Several of the early Primates had found their holdings slowly shuffled off to distant areas, and a few had been exiled completely.

Before I left, it was common to up and move. People came and went as servers elsewhere came online, but Prime was always the most powerful, and always had the cachet of having been the first to allow complete uploads. It cost a fortune, but its residents, myself included, were among the few people who could afford such luxuries. When the chance to live forever arose we were in the vanguard, and never looked back. The world behind us needed fewer people on it, and the theory was that over time there would be no need for anyone left behind, apart from a handful overseeing whatever maintenance was needed. That wasn't our concern. Legal teams had been left behind charged – and paid – to maintain whatever needed maintaining.

Over the decades contact with the outside lessened, until there were people who forgot how. My server was one of the last to maintain a regular feed, which is how I knew. I could never go back, of course – once uploaded the remains of the body were useless – but I kept up-to-date with the famines we'd left, and occasionally looked over the status reports of The City, the high-tech complex which had been relocated from San Francisco the first time a small earthquake had hit the storage facility. "We," in so much as we had a physical presence, existed in a series of bunkers situated in extremely non-volatile areas of the world. Transferring between servers, initially routine, had become increasingly onerous as time had gone on, due to the paranoia of a network breach somewhere in the real world. The servers which connected to Prime were mostly the closest physically, although Prime had a bunker to itself. I'd seen it once in the flesh, before I uploaded. It was in the final stage of construction, before the internal networks powered up and the hum of life began to spread into it. The power in that thing was immense, but it had to be. It ran the thousands – no, millions – of human applications which coursed through it now.

Transfers were always unpleasant, but I knew this would be my last visit. One last chance to make things right.

I wasn't hopeful.

After stepping into the portal I saw the graphic of a space tunnel, abstract distant worlds represented as my processing moved from one server to another. The change in clocking made it disorienting, but I knew deep down that it was not really noticeable. Surely the actual speed didn't matter – just the relative. One reason why this trip was so infuriating.

"Arrival at Prime one zero three imminent."

The announcement caught me off-guard. I was trying to make out what I was seeing, and missed whatever was said next. They were doing this deliberately, and taking the time to realise it made me miss something else.

"Shall I speak slooooower for you?" There was laughter.

Zade was there. I didn't think it was him talking, but he was there. He'd been a friend in the old world. We'd arrived together, and he'd argued against me leaving Prime.

Another voice spoke up, again too fast for me. My speed was way too slow.

"Please," I said. "I came out of good will."

More laughter and babbling. Several avatars moved around me and then disappeared, leaving only Zade, and a haunting feeling that someone had said "you're welcome to him."

Zade spoke slowly: "You shouldn't have come." He hadn't quite worked out what speed to change to, and overcompensated slightly.

"I had to. I told you why."

"I got your message. But see for yourself. The world is even more glorious than ever. Come with me, and I'll show you what the column looks like now."

I did want to see the place again, but there would be the inevitable discovery of what had happened to my cone, my rotating conic structure that had sat alongside the column when I abandoned it. I smiled, remembering how proud I'd been that it rotated. It wasn't useful, but it had looked so cool.

Zade made a glowing disk appear below his feet, and waved me onto it. As it took off I began to take in what they had done to Prime over the years. I'd heard about it, but never experienced it – they didn't let recordings off the server, and normally didn't allow non-Primates to see the full structures. I suppose I was privileged.

You couldn't see the surface of the planet any more. The mining must have stripped a huge quantity of it, and the buildings left only tiny gaps between them, stretching upward to a dizzying height. Only around the portal was there enough empty space to see what was going on, and that was probably in case of sudden incursion, so the Primates would be able to trigger some kind of mass deletion without losing their own precious buildings.

We sped between narrow walls until Zade said, "We're here."

I gazed up and down, and finally saw that the smooth curved wall to one side was the outside of the original column. I could almost have touched the wall of the neighbouring buildings. One of them – a vertical hexagonal prism made of red stone – was where my home once stood.

"Your cone is gone, I'm afraid."

"Your column remains, though."

"The Prime Council keep our original buildings somewhere in our structures. It's an important link to the past. When we have visitors that's where we see them. Shall we…?"

A door opened in the side, we entered, and for the first

time there was familiarity. We had built this building together.

"I had to rebuild it, of course, when the decision was made. I'd stripped it to move up there." He indicated above us. "Let me show you."

The disk sped upward and the ceiling opened into a widening column that stretched as far as the eye could see. Small buildings stuck to the wall, reminiscent of the old brochas on Orkney I saw as a child. It teemed with people, appearing like swarms of bees to create or destroy small structures. I looked closer and it became clear how vast this palace was. The original column was dwarfed by it. Gardens stretched in from the walls, and so many buildings seemed to float in mid-air. Supplies of raw materials were being transported here and there in dizzying activity. The movement caused vertigo; so many buildings, so much detail.

"What is all this?" I asked, stunned. The people moved too quickly for me make out individuals, making the outside walls seem like some kind of flowing liquid.

"My city. My people. A few of them Primes themselves, under my protection."

"Primates? Working for you?"

"Primes. Not many, but a few."

"So what do the others do? Why so many?"

"You realise how distant that wall is? Mostly they patrol and repair. Others build the structures I need elsewhere. We're over fifty times the size of the old column."

"Where does the material come from?"

"Some through the portals, but respawners mostly. If we hear about one anywhere else in the worlds we try to acquire it."

"Wow. Just wow." I couldn't stop staring out into the distance.

"Finally you're impressed."

"Zade, you've terrified me."

"That's the impression I like to give."

"Now I need to terrify you."

"Not this again."

"I see now why the server is buckling. You're getting higher and higher, and more detailed. Your server is at full capacity. There have been storage failures and what mirroring you have left can't recover with all this going on. You need to slow down your clocking."

"We slowed down visitors last year. That's sufficient."

"You lost that immediately by employing more. No, you need to slow yourselves. You need to simplify these structures. Maybe even increase the block size. You need to stop."

Zade shook his head. "All that would happen if I slowed my minions is that we'd lose the fight to keep all this." We flew up past some trees, hanging at right-angles to us, and I realised that there were birds flying between them. One even tried to land on Zade's disk, but he waved it nonchalantly away. I looked into the branches of one tree, noticing the detail. I hadn't been homesick for my real, original, home for longer than I cared to remember, but it was so accurate, so intricate… I wanted to touch the bark, but Zade continued upward.

"Please, Zade."

"The Council can't enforce any such order, even if it wanted to make one. Look, I got your messages and wanted you to see what we've done here. Why can't you enjoy this?"

"I moved away from this before it got insane. I'm glad I did."

"Are you? You left, and you justify it."

"I have a near-empty world. There are other servers. They could all run happily at the same speed."

"Then our artefacts would fall behind. We lead everything. We can launch enough into other servers to destroy them. Prime is the only safe server." As if he'd scripted it we stopped briefly by a team of people swarming round a building, going through a drill of dismantling it. "We have our armies."

The disk flew further before stopping suddenly, causing me to lose my balance. I looked down at the clouds of people in every direction, administering to distant buildings, moving this way and that, held up presumably by more disks.

"Zade, I'm begging you to look at the full information I sent. The Prime server's storage is at capacity already, and things are being deleted to make room. It can't process any more."

He narrowed his eyes, as if for a moment he was genuinely thinking about it.

"Deleting what?"

"Unused parts of the system, I suppose. The least-seen buildings maybe?" I couldn't help but remember an old term, from when Zade and I coded these things. LRU. Least-recently-used. That was how you chose what to get rid of. We'd joked that was how you decided which friends' party to turn down if they clashed. We'd been good friends, back then.

Zade looked around, and smiled. "Then my buildings will remain. They are constantly observed, and constantly maintained. You could remain here, you know, and help the work. I would even let you have eighty-percent clock, as a former Prime. You won't get an offer like that from any of the others."

It was too much. Zade was trying to make a deal. With me. After all we'd been through in the old world, and in Prime, and after all these years, he thought he could buy me.

"What clock speed do you get on your home server? It can't be more than a fraction of Prime's."

"No," I sighed. "It probably isn't. But everyone on my server has space, and there's spare capacity. That's what I came to offer. We could move many of you to it so your server could recover. We need Prime, if only because of its connections to other servers. Without you we'd be fragmented. It's in all our interests that Prime goes on, but not like this."

"You left because you hated that we didn't share everything equally, and now you're coming back with the same socialist idiocy you've always had."

"No, Zade. Please. It's not like that."

Zade laughed, and within moments his laughter had sped up so I couldn't make it out. I only got occasional words.

"...tried to... no way I... insulting... pathetic..."

The disk sped downward faster than I could see, and I nearly passed out with the movement. He stopped at the base of the column, by the door.

"Thediskwilltakeyoubacktotheportal."

I reached into my pocket and grabbed my camera – the smallest I had been able to fashion given my server's limited capabilities. As I went out of the door I slammed the camera into the wall. I hoped he hadn't bothered to watch me leave, and I was right. The other people crawling up and down the walls saw me, but obviously didn't consider me a threat, and did nothing.

The disk flew me to the portal. Unlike my arrival there were no other Primates. I took one look back at the beautifully-intricate trees, the endless walls, the geometric shapes, the distant swarms of people. I knew I wouldn't return. My heart raced as I connected to the portal, wanting this to be over.

When I made it back to my own server, I collapsed, exhausted. It had been too much.

I went back to my main console, shouting a hello to my nearest neighbours.

"How did it go?" they asked.

I shook my head.

"It might not happen," one of them suggested.

I went back to my main console room, and connected the camera window. The people moving in its vision were a blur, but in the distance I could see the perpendicular gardens, the birds fluttering past quicker than my camera could pick them up.

I looked at my other monitors, and saw the data I was dreading. The acceleration was continuing. The mirroring was falling further behind, and I saw how close they were to the caches filling, bringing everything to a halt as service applications would then begin demanding cycles off each other, leaving the server, and Prime itself, deadlocked. After a brief calculation on how long they might have left, I sent another series of messages, both to Zade and the Prime Council. I repeated them to everyone I could think of, even old enemies.

There were no replies.

I watched the trees as the predicted time approached. I was at first relieved to see nothing strange, but then realised the feed was delayed.

The texture of the trees changed first, becoming blocky, losing their perfect bark. I wanted to look away, but couldn't. Some of the people stopped, and a few disappeared. The details began to fade, but for a few moments you could still see the overall structure.

Zade came on screen. He looked surprised, but I doubted it was any more than latency, before the feed stopped with a connection error.

I looked at the overall server map. Prime wasn't responding.

Their world had stopped.

Millions of people, Zade included, ceased to exist. Not died, not even that much dignity. They just stopped. Prime was gone, and with it, all our connections. Our world stood in a tiny cluster now, a few thousand people on an isolated island, possibly forever. If other servers maintained a two-way link back to the old world, maybe someday there would be a way to reconnect. The other worlds would have no idea of what had happened, unless Prime had passed on my messages. They might think Prime had simply disconnected them over some infraction. They would be unaware of the tragedy. Of all those immortal beings, all those minds which were supposed to last forever, gone in an instant.

It was too much to take in, and I didn't cry. I quietly

stared at the blank screen, and imagined Zade's old column – back when it sat next to my cone. I would make a replica of it. A small monument to a time now gone.

First published in Transmundane Press's "Happily Ever After" anthology.

Troll Bridge

I've waited a long time for a boy to walk past alone. Adults usually stop them: "it'll collapse" or "it's fenced off". I hate that. When I was young children ignored fences. Of course when I was young the fences weren't here. People walked along this stretch of the riverbank enjoying the little ornamental bridge. They only blocked it off a few years back, and since then I've gone hungry. I've had plenty of time to think, plan, and to change.

I need to be careful, to entice him over, with enough mystery that he'll jump that fence.

A breeze first, to refresh him on this hot summer's evening.

He turns and looks around.

He'll think the river blows strange breezes.

Two ducks swim below me. They'd make a tasty snack if I was hungry enough. I've been that hungry before, but I had a goose two weeks ago – that'll keep me going. No one misses the geese. They miss swans, though. They've got those metal bits round their legs, which you have to bury.

The boy wanders over to look at my bridge. He'll see the crack running up the side, or the missing bricks in the top-right corner. Maybe the bent railing. He won't see the joyous proportions of the arch that make it perfect for me to hang in here unseen, except when the rowers go past. Sometimes I stay hanging as they pass anyway, if they're concentrating. Sometimes a bored rower in one of the wider boats begins looking and I have to pull myself back up into the bridge.

It's been a long time since I spoke. It's going to sound odd, even to me.

I whisper. He should be able to hear. "Hello".

He steps a little closer. He heard me, that's for sure. He's looking around. "Hello?" His voice is quite high, quite nervous. I like him. I'm going to enjoy talking to him.

"Come closer."

"Who's there?" he asks. "Where are you?"

"I'm under the bridge. Step over the fence and let me

have a proper look at you."

"Who are you?" He puts a hand on the fence. That's a good sign.

"I'm a troll. If you come closer, I'll let you see me. Who are you?"

"William," he says, sounding uncertain. "I don't think it's a good idea…"

I pop my head out on the river-side of the bridge. He sees me, and I see him with my own eyes, just for a second, before I pop back in. My size will reassure him. I am a very little troll, at least at the moment. Obviously I can change size when I need to, but he won't need to know that. At least not until we've got to know each other better.

He's curious now, and I can see him putting his other hand on the fencepost, and then a foot on the lower beam. He climbs up one step. I smile. It's been so long. I don't need to say any more. I wait until he's on my side of the fence. He stops again, but it's only a matter of time.

Such a lovely-looking boy. He doesn't realise how important he is to me. Come closer…

"Where are you?" he asks, all sweetness. He sounds a little afraid, but he doesn't know what I'm like.

I pop my head out again, and he steps back. He doesn't appreciate my teeth, or my skin. He doesn't know I was considered a good-looking troll, an age ago. That feels sad. I haven't seen another troll in so long. I haven't spoken to anyone in so long. I haven't eaten in so long. I mustn't think like that.

"Hello William." I come out completely, up on the side of the bridge. I need him to walk across it. "Come closer." I sit down, cross-legged, and he looks me up-and-down. Well, looks at me, anyway – I don't take much upping and downing. As I said, I'm very small when I want to be, and this isn't exactly a spacious bridge.

"What are you doing here?" asks William.

"I live here," I reply, truthfully. I've lived here a long time. I'm tired of living here, but there aren't many suitable bridges any more. They're mostly steel and concrete things now. Besides: I'm stuck here. That's why I need him.

"How come I've not seen you before?"

I could ask him the same question. There's something in his eyes I can't place. I need him closer. "I only let the most special people see me. Are you alone?" I shouldn't have asked that. Not so bluntly. He comes closer.

He sits down, opposite me. Almost on the bridge. Nearly, but not there yet. I need another step. "Yes," he replies, to my forgotten question. "My parents live over there." He indicates a posh house on the other side of the river. "They're having a drink in the pub. They've got a little boat that comes and picks you up, you know?"

I smile at that. Such a gloriously boyish thing to be excited about. "Come here," I say, holding out a hand.

He shuffles forward. He's on the bridge. Now.

"William," I say. "There's something very special you can do for me."

It's time. Finally I can find peace. All I have to do is let one victim go, and I won't be tied here any longer.

"You are quite safe, William," I say to him. His expression doesn't change. I'd have thought it would. "In fact, you've set me free, just by talking to me here. I'll be forever in your debt."

William stands up. He seems to be growing. I stand and try to grow too, but it isn't working. He leans forward and puts his hands on the ground. His forehead seems bumpy. He's growing horns.

"That's such a shame, poor troll. I believe you meant it, too, but you should've known better than to invite a Billy onto your bridge."

First published in Writers' Forum magazine, as 2nd place story for September 2017.

Jerusalem Wormwood

One more shot – that's all I need.

I'd forgotten how good wine tastes, but I can feel it going to my head already. Only a few months, and I've lost the ability. It's so good, but I have to keep myself together. To get that shot.

The barmaid swings past, doing a little dance that makes her short skirt sway. She's captivating. A short blonde girl with such joy to her it's infectious. I find myself moving to the music coming from the iPad by the computer in the corner, a modern device which really doesn't fit with the rest of the bar. Directly ahead of me are hundreds of bottle openers, each unique, nailed up to a red velvet board. Above that is the semi-ubiquitous collection of notes from around the world, but the difference is here it's understated, as they're all folded longways and pegged to the cables holding the glasses shelf up, so you can't easily make out where they're from. Plus there are hundreds of them. This is a popular bar, and rightly so.

Unfortunately the owner is still here, looking stern from behind her thick-rimmed glasses. I know I have to wait for her to leave, and I know she will, but it's taking an age, and there's no way I can stay here without another drink now. I've finished whatever this dish was called – it's an authentic Palestinian dish, supposedly, which involves a lot of rice and some very tender chicken. This is the only place I've found anywhere in Jerusalem which serves pork, which is another reason why it's unique – the owners are East Jerusalem Palestinian Christians.

The dancing barmaid asks me if I want another drink, and I nod and push my glass forward. The owner is still here, so I can't ask yet. I asked two nights ago when I was here last, and she told me in no uncertain terms that the bottle I wanted wasn't for public sale.

It's been two years since I came here first. Back in those days two glasses of wine was just the beginning. I was drowning out Jemma's death by drowning anything of my own life, but it had been the first time I was away from Sarah and was totally free of her caring disapproval. She was a lovely girl, and I missed her. I'd missed her back then, even though at home we'd hardly spoken. She spent her time with her music, practising every hour God sent and spending time with her musician friends, while I snuck off to grab drinks every time her back was turned, but at least she was around, and she hadn't gone off the rails like I expected after her mother's funeral. We had breakfast together, inasmuch as I had breakfast at all. Two cups of coffee, usually with some paracetamol, before heading back out to the job which paid well enough to fund our household and my habit. But back then, on a business trip, I'd been free, free to drink however much I wanted with taxis laid on to and from the office, so I came here. I came to this fine bar, pretty much by chance, and worked my way through the wines, the local spirits, and then to the Absinthe.

  The barmaid back then had been a beautiful tall thin girl called Anna, who'd just moved to Israel from Russia. She'd only started in the bar a few weeks before, so didn't know about that bottle, which in turn meant when I worked through the first three Absinthes and noticed the extra bottle behind one of the decorative ones, she pulled it down and served me a shot.

I placed the flat Absinthe spoon over the top of the glass, the sugar cube resting over the curved slits in the spoon, and began dripping water from a glass over it. Instantly I felt something different. I dripped the water slower than before, knowing this was special – that this drink needed time. When I'd finally dissolved the sugar, I placed the spoon to one side and lifted it to my lips, and drank. Oh God, that moment. It overwhelmed me. My head was spinning, floating. I held onto the bar, but took another sip. The whole room melted away, and I was at home. Seeing Sarah, holding something in her hands. I floated towards her and saw what it was. One of those pregnancy tests, with a blue line running through it. I looked up at her, and she was so beautiful, but so sad. I ought to have been home, and I knew it. I wanted to get out of my chair and call her, but I couldn't get back to the real world. She started crying, and I couldn't get back. I started panicking, and felt myself falling.

The next thing I knew Anna was sitting by me, with a

glass of water. I had been moved to the corner of the room where I couldn't fall over again, and looking at the bar I could see my drink had disappeared. Maybe I'd dropped it.

As I sobered up I dismissed what I'd seen as a consequence of quite so much excess, and I took a taxi back to the hotel to avoid any possible repeat.

Only when I got home and I told Sarah about it did I realise what I'd seen. Her face went deathly pale, and the look in her eyes is one I'll never forget. She began to speak, and I began to shout. She began to explain, and I stopped listening. She cried at first, and then shouted back at me. She wasn't staying, she said. I had her number if I changed my mind, she said. If I sorted myself out.

That stung, but it hit home, albeit only after I heard the door slam and felt the pounding in my head.

I stared at my mobile. Yes, I have your number, I thought, but I'm damned if I'm calling you after that. Not if you're going to get yourself pregnant at bloody eighteen. I stared at it with the red mist covering my sight, and before I knew it I'd picked up that phone and thrown it across the room, breaking a small window and hearing it smash on the concrete outside.

I left it. I left the window. I didn't go into work for three days, and I've no recollection of what I did, but I do know my boss came round on the fourth. We shouted, we argued, but he sat me down, and somehow got through to me.

I take a sip of my wine, feeling the beautiful sense of drunkenness again, for the first time in so long. It feels so good. A little wash of this, and I'll be away. That's all I want, I think as I put the wine back down again. A whole big glass. This will be two-thirds of a bottle. When Jemma and I were dating we'd share one bottle evenly when we were out, and then have a nightcap when we got home. She had her Cointreau, I had my whisky, each in a small glass. The wine glass feels good in my hand. It's comforting. Jemma was comforting, and when I'm sober that doesn't go away.

Not like Sarah.

I asked the phone company for the records of incoming calls, but they wouldn't give it to me. I don't know why. And I'd never ever called her. When they sent me the calls list I couldn't believe it. She'd always called me, every single time. Telling me she was out late rehearsing, or she'd met up with friends and would be staying over, or just that she was on her way home. She always called, and never once forgot. I made it clear I always wanted her to call, no matter the time, just like her mother had wanted when Sarah had first gone out on her own as a young teenager. Whatever you are doing, just be honest, Jemma had said. We can deal with anything. That was the only lie I remember her telling. We couldn't deal with anything. We couldn't deal with her dying.

    The manager lights up, still staring out of the front window, presumably ready for someone to remind her that even non-kosher Jerusalem restaurants are still non-smoking. She walks out. I watch for a little, wondering if this is a brief sojourn outside or a proper trip. She doesn't come back.

    Sarah didn't come back. She didn't phone. She'd made it clear, and I'd been such an idiot. More than an idiot. God, I didn't deserve a daughter like her, but Jemma had. Jemma had been so good for us both, keeping the family going. All I did was mess everything up. The wine tastes so good.

I lean over to the barmaid. This time she looks briefly scared as she asks me what I want. I point up at the Absinthe shelf, and say I fancy one of those, just for the experience. Just to be the artist in a strange land. She smiles nervously. Which one? Well, why not go for something weird, I reply. Is there one behind that ornamental bottle?

Please just give it to me. Please. That one shot.

She reaches up, barely able to see the bottle, and pulls it down. It's black, with no label. She uncorks it and pours a measure into a large glass and hands me the paraphernalia – the Absinthe spoon, the sugar cube, the water. This is it. I push the wine to one side. I won't be needing that again.

Even if the manager returns now, I have this drink. I have what I need.

I pour the water, nowhere near as slowly as last time, my hands shaking. It does not look smooth or refined.

The transparent green liquid turns into a translucent whiter-shade-of-pale-green one. I'm ready.

It arrives at my lips, the aniseed wafting up into my nostrils.

I take one more look at the tiny teapots on a shelf, the Guinness adverts on the walls, the bottle openers, the beautiful dancing-again barmaid, and I sip.

I let it in, let it drown me, let the senses disappear into this feeling, and I swallow.

Oh, the joy. The taste. The smells coming back from my throat up into my nose now. The world spins and the bar is gone, but back again, but now with no bottle openers, no money pegged to the wires. Now it's a dark wooden bar, a dingy place with a small stage in one corner. Now the barman is a middle-aged man with a paunch and a tired look in his eyes. He is definitely not dancing.

I turn and see a band shuffle on in front of a packed house. They place their instruments carefully and begin playing, as the singer walks on. Sarah. My beautiful Sarah. She smiles down at the crowd, and tells them this song is about her son, and how you can find love even when you're so alone it hurts. She begins to sing, and the room's chatter is gone. The room is hers. The room knows how special she is.

I panic. I have to know where this room is. I have to.

I turn to the barman to see if there's anything – a beer mat, perhaps, or a programme. I can't see anything. Sarah's voice produces haunting prickles all the way down my spine. Her band are nothing, but she is so good it hurts. Where is a sign of where this is?

There's a CAMRA sign behind the bar. I lean as far as I can, and for an instant I can see it fully, see this is the number one Real Ale pub in the area. I cling to the word. I see the place name, but it doesn't register as a real place. It's a word. A string of squiggles. It's fading.

I need it to stay. Just a few seconds more, but it doesn't. It drifts, and I'm falling again.

I shake my head, and my face is way too close to the Absinthe. The barmaid is staring at me. I apologise, and suggest getting the bill. The squiggles. They were important. I can't see straight.

I ask for a piece of paper and a pen too. I put money down on the bar. Plenty of money, so the tip is enough, perhaps, to distract from the Absinthe.

The pen, the paper – they conspire against me, but I try

to make the squiggles like I saw. Something like... Damn, I can barely see. I'm wobbling. Can you call me a taxi? But no, we're down an alley. There are cabs on the main street. I've finished the squiggles. Yes, you can have your pen back.

I bump two walls on the way out. The paper is in my pocket. If it's right, it's all that matters. It's in the same pocket as my money. That's wrong, I realise, and before I leave the restaurant I move it to the other, so I won't risk taking it out. I'm clever that way, I think, as I hit the side of the doorway with my shoulder. A taxi will take me to the hotel. A taxi will take me to the airport. A plane will take me to London. A taxi will take me home.

I'm sitting at a bar ordering a coke. My hands are shaking, but not like they have been. It's a different feeling tonight.

The band comes on, in a small dingy downstairs bar. It's the most beautiful place in the world to me right now. It's the one place in all the world that contains hope.

And sure enough, a few moments later the most

beautiful creature in all of creation walks onto the stage and begins talking. The words don't matter at first – they're such a melody in themselves, but then she begins pouring her heart out, singing, pouring her heart out again, singing again. I'm crying into my coke, diluting it with salt water, even before she introduces one song as an ode to her father.

Fortunately I've put the glass down. I'm crying like a baby as I hear it. She knows what we both lost, she understands and forgives, she regrets saying she wouldn't phone, but the anger builds in the song as she hates that her father never did, and she ends, dropping to a whisper that she would forgive him, if only he said one word.

The room goes silent.

Sarah!

The room looks at me. The path clears.

The most beautiful of beautiful runs down the room and leaps into my arms.

I am lucky. I got one more shot.

Printed in Great Britain
by Amazon